JESSIE'S GIRL

NAIMA SIMONE

PROLOGUE

Asa

"You knew."

I stare at the woman standing on my front porch. It's almost midnight, and though it's the last week of October and the air carries a bite with razor-sharp teeth, she's clothed in nothing but a thin, long-sleeved T-shirt and skinny jeans ripped at the thigh and knees. She's shown up unannounced on my doorstep in the middle of the night, looking as if she just threw on clothes, ran out of the house, and jumped in the car.

Yet, I don't ask India Roberts what she's doing here or what she wants.

And I don't ask her what she means by her cryptic "you knew."

Because she's right. I know.

One look into those wide but shattered penny-brown eyes, and I know.

Instead of answering, I step back and hold the door open wider, silently inviting her to come in. She doesn't release me from her gaze as she steps into my house, and part of me wishes she would. For my sake.

Because she's ripping me to bloody, jagged shreds with those eyes. Eyes that should only shine with delight, laughter, and love, but are now so dark with pain it's like looking into an abyss.

I close the door behind her, and she slowly turns around to face me. And that's how we stand in the small foyer—my arms down at my sides and hers crossed over her chest. Friends turned adversaries, hovering on either side of an imaginary line drawn in the proverbial sand.

Me, the betrayer. Her, the betrayed.

At least in her eyes.

"You knew," she accuses again, in that hoarse voice that sounds as if a carpenter took several feet of sandpaper to it.

"It wasn't mine to tell." My voice, even and deep, doesn't reveal how there's an angry, wounded animal howling inside me. It's demanding I go to her, wrap myself around her like a living blanket to soak up the hurt, that agony that damn near vibrates in her husky tone.

"Wasn't yours to tell?" she repeats. A harsh, hollow bark of laughter follows as she tips her head back and stares at the ceiling for a brief moment. When she looks at me again, anger flickers, mingling bright and hot with the pain. "You were supposed to be my friend."

"I am, India." The fingers of my right hand curl into a fist. One I wish I could plow into the nearest wall. Or my best friend Jessie's face. "I am your friend. Never doubt that."

"Yeah," she scoffs, her full mouth with its plump bottom lip twisting into a bitter caricature of a smile. "That's why you let me walk around with my head up my ass for how long? You let me live a lie. You let me be *a fool*." She shakes her head so hard, her dark brown, tight curls brush her cheekbones. "And for the life of me, I can't figure out which one is worse. Finding out the man I loved—the life I lived with him—was a figment of my dumb ass Pollyanna imagination. Or that I was a willfully blind idiot, and everyone I trusted was in on the joke. The joke being me."

"Baby girl," I murmur, risking her wrath, her disgust, and stepping across that line in the sand to stand in front of her. To... touch her.

I've been very careful about touching this woman. Brief hugs. Deliberate but friendly distance. Even a fucking pat on the head. But now, with her hurt beating off of her in red-tinged waves, I can't *not* put my hands on her. Even if it's just her slim shoulders. But it might as well be on those just-less-than-a-handful and utterly perfect breasts. Or those feminine, rounded hips. Or that ripe peach of an ass.

It doesn't matter where my palms skate or where my fingertips press into her gleaming chestnut skin. It's all sexual. It's all dirty.

Because it's all her.

For me, it's always been her.

My fantasy. My sin.

My joy. My regret.

My best friend's woman.

Jessie's girl.

She bats my hands away from her, whirling around to pace to the other side of my small foyer. Which takes about four steps before she's headed back my way. Her arms cradle her chest as if they're the only things holding her together. If she uncrossed them, she might splinter into pieces all over my dark hardwood floor.

"Jessie told you tonight?" I ask, studying her,

wanting to stop her frenetic motion, but I've risked putting my hands on her once. No way in hell am I chancing it again. Besides, the way she jerked out of my hold, she would probably claw and scratch my fucking eyes out if I tried to touch her again.

She shakes her head, another of those horrible, empty chuckles escaping her. "No, he didn't tell me. His side-chick DM'd me. She decided it was high time I found out about her existence. For my own good, you see. She thought it only right that I knew what my long-time boyfriend was up to when he wasn't with me. And just in case I didn't believe her, she provided pictures."

What a thoughtful bitch.

She stutters to a stop, rocking slightly on the balls of her feet. "Oh *God*. I'll never be able to... to..." Her harsh gasps shred the air, her chest rising and falling with each ragged inhale. She rubs her fists against her eyes, for a moment appearing like a young girl instead of a twenty-four-year-old woman. "I'll never be able to scrub those images from my head. How could he..."

She doesn't finish, but she doesn't need to.

I've asked myself the same question thousands of times since Jessie confessed to me a couple of weeks ago about his drunken one-night stand with a football groupie. He'd been broken—the closest I'd ever seen my best friend come to crying. And he'd been terrified about India finding out. Terrified he'd lose her. I felt for him—I did. Given my own history of growing up with a gambler father who saw women as poker chips to be won, cashed in, then doled out to his bitch-ass buddies, cheating was a deal breaker for me. No excuses.

But Jessie's transgression seemed even more of a betrayal.

Because it was India. He had this woman's loyalty. Her body. Her heart. And he'd tossed it all aside to get his dick wet in some random's pussy.

Yes, I loved him, and I promised not to tell India so he could do it first. But a part of me... a part of me hated the man I'd been best friends with since Jacob Parsons broke Jessie's glasses in the fourth grade, and I broke that bully bastard's front tooth with my fist.

I resented Jessie for throwing away what I would've gift-wrapped and hand-delivered my soul to the devil to have.

"He loves you, India," I murmur. Because as his best friend, I have to fight for him... fight for them. And I know it's the truth. "He fucked up, but he would die for you."

"Don't you dare defend him," she whispers low and fierce, whipping around to face me. "He would die for me, but he can't quite manage to keep his dick in his pants and out of other women?" She sliced a hand through the air. "I don't need that kind of love. Fuck. His. Love."

Wasn't shit I could say to that. I agree with her, and while I might be the worst friend since Brutus, I'm not a hypocrite. I wouldn't convince her to give him another chance when I would never offer a woman a second opportunity to stab me in the back.

Watched that shit happen with my parents on repeat like it was goddamn Groundhog's Day when I was a kid. Had it happen to me when I was foolish enough to trust my heart with someone, only to have them twist and pound it like Play-Doh.

Maybe that's why I need India to be with Jessie. As long as she's his woman, she's unattainable, untouchable. I can fantasize about her while my dick throbs and jerks in my fist, secretly crave that cocktease of a body, and hunger for the beautiful smile capable of lighting up a city skyline. But I can't have her because she's my best friend's girl. Which means I can't fall for her.

In other words, she's safe.

Goddammit, I *need* her to be safe.

Her sigh ripples in the air. Closing her eyes, she pinches the bridge of her nose. When she lowers her hand and lifts her lashes, her grief, her pain gut punches me. Jesus Christ.

"India," I rasp.

"I'm not naïve," she says, all the agony in her chocolate eyes thickening her voice. "I know about the lifestyle of athletes. Especially when they're on the road more than they're home. And with me teaching, it's not like I can just drop everything and travel with him. But I got all that. I was prepared for the women throwing themselves at him on social media and even right in front of me. All of it goes with the territory of being a professional football player. But somehow," her voice cracks and her frame quakes in a full-body tremor, "somehow, I thought we were above that. Stupidly, I thought our biggest hurdle would be keeping our lines of communication open. Not other women. Never other women. Why would he give away what should've been just for me? Should've been just for us? How could he touch another woman like he touched me? Did it mean so little? Did *I* mean..."

She doesn't finish the sentence. And I don't know if it's because she can't bear to complete the thought... or if it's my arms crushing her to me. My hands thrusting into her hair, tangling, and pressing her face to my chest.

My rules of no-contact shatter under the weight of her pain and that sacrilegious trace of insecurity in her voice. There's no way I can stand there and *not* hold her. Fuck, I want to absorb her pain into my body, have it mark my skin like tattoos and wear them proudly. More than anything, though, I only want to take that pain away from her.

As if the press of my body to hers unlocks a rusty gate, her grief erupts in a ragged torrent of sobs. They tear into her petite frame, and the shudders echo through me like the discordant notes of an out-of-tune guitar. Loud. Harsh. Raw. *Jesus*, how can her bones not snap under the strength of them? How is she still in one piece? Irrational fear stabs me in the chest, and I tighten my arms around her. I curl around her, burying my face in her curls, widening my legs to draw her even closer. I surround her, determined to hold her together. To not let her break.

I don't keep track of how long I hold her. Minutes feel like hours, and they both pass like seconds. At some point, we sink to the floor, and I cradle her on my lap. Senseless murmurs spill from my lips. *I got you. It's going to be okay. You're breaking my heart, baby girl.* Senseless because I can't have her—I can *never* have her. And I doubt anything will be the same after this, much less okay.

After a while, her sobs soften, the emotional storm easing. But she doesn't move away from me, and God help me, I don't loosen my arms from around her. I'm a greedy bastard, and after depriving myself of this pleasure for so long, I'm clinging to it as long as she allows it. Allows me.

With every moment that passes, all of my senses kick into a higher mode. As if, until now, I've been living in black and white, but the press of her body to mine catapults me into my own Land of Oz, and I'm seeing in brilliant Technicolor for the first time.

Each small hitch in her breath tugs on my heart. My eyes note the spiked length of her wet lashes and the faint tremble of her mouth. God, I want to sweep my thumb over that pouty, too-damn-sexy-for-my-sanity bottom lip. Test its give and firmness. Then assess it again with my tongue. Her scent, a heady combination of the jasmine oil she's obsessed with and fresh rain after a spring storm, infiltrates my nose, floods my mouth and I swear, I can taste it. My gut spasms, hungry for that taste.

She's the fucking hottest IMAX experience sitting right here on my thighs.

India tips her head back against my shoulder, and her copper gaze brands me.

"Thank you," she whispers, and I almost wince in sympathy at the rawness of her voice.

"You're welcome."

Without my conscious permission, my fingers find her throat, gently massage the front where her vocal cords run. She swallows and the up-and-down motion bobs against my fingertips. Something so innocuous, so mundane, and yet it strikes a match to the desire-infused fuel in my veins, and I light up like fire set to dry kindle.

My heart pounds against my sternum like an anvil, ringing in my ears. My thighs tighten under her ass, and my cock. Fuck, my cock is so hard, I ache. With her petite, deliciously thick body perched on my lap, need and pain are so intertwined, separating them would be like trying to shift sand into color groups. Next to impossible.

How can she not notice? How can she not feel—

Her eyes widen and a low, almost hushed gasp pierces the air between us. And I have my answer. She does notice. She does feel.

Goddamn it.

For three years I've kept my dirty, fucked-up lust for her a secret. She's my best friend's girl, has only had eyes for him since the moment they met during an event at the elementary school where she taught. I'm a grease monkey with more real life experience than college education. That can't compare to a professional football player with a fuck ton of zeroes in his bank account. To India, I am and always will be her man's friend, his brother-by-choice.

And no matter how many times I've imagined her watching me with those eyes full of need and the knowledge that only I can satisfy it... No matter how many times I've envisioned her loving me with that body created to be worshipped and corrupted... No matter how many times I've dreamed of holding her during the dark hours of night... Yeah, no matter how I've betrayed Jessie over and over again in my head, I've never given either India or him any clue of how much I crave her. It's been my only consolation.

But now I no longer have even that tiny comfort. Or shred of pride.

Jaw clenched, I drop my hands to her hips, prepared to move her off me.

"Asa," she breathes, her gaze searching mine, questioning.

"You okay now?" Cutting her off, I tighten my grip on her and am already pushing her away from me. And ignoring the inquiry in her eyes. What the hell could I say? *Yes, my dick is hard for you while you cry over your boyfriend. And that makes me a piece of shit.*

As far as I'm concerned, it's understood. No need for it to be spoken aloud.

"Asa." Small, delicate hands cup my face, paralyzing me.

I can't move, can't fucking breathe as she shifts, straddles my legs. Jesus Christ. Jesus Christ. What is she doing? Panic batters me, and my breath claws its way up my throat. How can she not see she's killing me? Torturing me?

Somehow, I force my arms to move when the rest of me is still trapped in a deep freeze. Mechanically, I replace my hands at her hips and with the strength of a newborn, I try again to shove her away. Off of me. Out of my house.

Out of my goddamn mind.

"Asa, look at me." Not until the moment she issues her softly spoken order and I obey, do I realize I'd closed my eyes. And that I'm shaking beneath her like an addict plummeting down from his first hit.

I'm a six-foot-three, two-hundred-pound mechanic who can bench press a transmission from a '69 Chevelle. And here I sit, trembling under a woman damn near half my size. Terrified. Of what she sees. Of what I feel. Of what I'm capable of if she doesn't get away from me.

Still not freeing me from her gaze, she smooths her thumbs over my cheekbones. Back and forth. Back and forth. Calming me. Searing me. Then slowly, so damn slowly, she lowers her head. And brushes her mouth over mine.

Shock, pleasure, and pain jolt me, and my body jerks as if electrocuted. A sound that's part animal, part human rumbles in my chest, scratches its way up my throat. It's desperate, agonized, and so, so fucking hungry.

Not heeding that sound as the warning it is, India sweeps her lips over mine again. Firmer this time. The tip of her tongue making an appearance and dipping into the corner of my mouth.

I snap.

The audile crack reverberates against my skull, and it's my control splintering.

With a growl, I snatch my hands from her waist and plunge them into her tight curls, fisting the dark strands. Her breath catches against my mouth, and that tiny sound, that small puff over my skin, incinerates any remnants of restraint I had left.

I take her mouth.

Own it.

Defile it.

One thrust of my tongue between her lips, and I'm lost. In her sultry taste. In all that wet warmth. In *her*. This kiss should be hesitant, uncertain. I may have fantasized about this with my fist choking my cock, but it's my first time with my mouth against hers. My tongue inside her.

I devour her like it's the hundredth time. Like my job, my fucking life's purpose, is to suck on that lush bottom lip that has tormented me for years. To lick the roof of her mouth before tangling my tongue with hers, coaxing her to play with me even while demanding she let me fuck this gorgeous mouth.

A harsh, dark sound rises up between us. A groan. A plea. And I'm not sure if it's from her throat or mine. I don't give a fuck. Not when her hands are tunneling through my hair, nails scraping my scalp. The same faint pinpricks that tingle over my head travel through my body and dance down my cock.

She tugs on my hair, and my hips surge in reply. A "yes." A "give it to me." A "don't you fucking stop."

The next sound that breaks on the air is definitely hers. It's a needy whimper. My blood pumps scalding hot through me, and every cell in my body heeds that unspoken request. Gripping her curls tighter, I drag her head to the side and deepen the kiss. Take more. And I buck between her legs, rolling my dick over her denim-covered pussy.

"Asa." Her soft cry vibrates against my lips, shakes against my ears.

And it's a blast of frigid water, drenching me. Ripping me from the vortex of lust I catapulted us both into and dumping me into cold, hard, unforgivable reality.

What the hell am I doing? Who the hell have I *become*?

This woman turned to me for answers, for comfort after finding out her man cheated, and I took advantage of it. I'm kissing my best friend's girl. I'm dry-fucking her on my foyer floor.

My actions are no better than his. Because I'm betraying her.

I'm betraying him. The man who has been closer to me than a brother since we were ten years old.

Who have I become? A vulture, scavenging and feeding on the carrion of their relationship.

Jesus Christ.

Pleasure had soaked her cry only seconds ago, but now as I thrust her away from me, it's filled with surprise. I tried to be gentle, but as she skids several inches on her ass across the brown laminate flooring, I know I failed in that. Regret for my careless handling spears through me, mingling in a noxious mix with the guilt, shame, and anger at myself.

"Fuck." I jackknife to my feet and crossing the short distance to cup her arm and tug her to her feet. After steadying her, I step back. And then again. Placing much needed space between us. Because my trust in myself spikes at a negative five. "I'm sorry. I didn't mean—" Grinding my teeth together, I scrub a hand down my face, forcing myself to meet her gaze. It's the least I can do. The very least. "I shouldn't have..." *Goddammit.* Can I get one whole fucking sentence out? "I'm sorry." I finally finish. Pathetically.

She stares at me, lifting two fingers to her kiss-swollen mouth, her copper eyes inscrutable. Part of me is glad for it—glimpsing the disgust and remorse there would punch a hole in my chest. But the other part... It's dying to know what she's thinking. Dying to know if she hates me for taking what wasn't mine. The *not* knowing—it's fucking killing me.

"Sorry," she repeats, dropping her arm to her side. An emotion that my frozen mind can't decipher flickers across her face. Pain. Regret. Disappointment... Resignation. Maybe a screwed-up combination of them all. "That seems to be going around, doesn't it?"

Shaking her head, she spins around and heads for the front door. The sight of her retreating back unlocks my muscles, and I lurch forward to... what? Stop her? Touch her? Apologize again? Beg her not to go? All of those ideas are epically bad.

"India." She pauses at the door, her hand gripping the knob. "I..." *Fuck.* "I'm so goddamn sorry." *Please forgive me.*

"You said that," she says, tone flat, empty. "And I hear you. Finally, I'm hearing and getting it. All of it."

With those cryptic words, she opens the doors and quietly shuts it. But I flinch, the soft snick as deafening as if she'd slammed it.

How long I stand there, staring at that door, my heart a hammer against my rib cage, I don't know. But one thing is for certain.

Touching India Roberts was a mistake. The biggest one I've ever made.

But the guilt flaying me alive isn't because I now know what my best friend's woman tastes like.

It's because, if given the chance to repeat that mistake, I'm not sure if I wouldn't do it again.

And damn the consequences.

1

TWO YEARS LATER

Asa

My cell phone vibrates against my hip, the ringtone assaulting my ears. Cursing, I push myself from underneath the side of the 2000 5.0 Mustang, the wheels of the creeper rolling smoothly over the cement of the mechanic shop's floor. Once I clear the undercarriage, I push to my feet. Impatience rides me as I snatch the phone from my jeans pocket. I've been working on pulling out the drive shaft so I can put in the universal joint, and since this particular customer is a fanatic about his car and a bit of an asshole, I want it done as soon as possible. I don't need this distraction.

But Lizzo telling someone the truth hurts means only one thing.

I swipe my thumb over the cell's screen, silencing the ringtone.

"Rose, what's wrong?" Because if my ten-year-old niece is calling me at one o'clock in the middle of a school day, something is definitely wrong.

Color me surprised.

When *isn't* something wrong?

"Uncle Asa, it's not my fault," Rose wails in my ear.

Before I can answer, another voice joins the conversation in the background. "Rose, I told you I would call your uncle. Hand over the phone."

Squeezing my eyes closed, I pinch the bridge of my nose. *Shit.* I know that voice. Am very familiar with it since I've heard it several times this school year—and it's only October. The principal, Mrs. Reyes, and I have a love-hate relationship. I love when a day goes by and her number doesn't pop up on my phone, and she hates to see me coming. Because when she does see me, it means my niece is in her office for whatever bullshit and mayhem Rose decided to let loose on any given day. Fourth grade, and already has her own personalized seat in the principal's office.

Just... fuck.

My older sister died a little over a year ago in a car accident, and for some unfathomable reason she named me as her daughter's guardian. I love my niece —adore her—but, I'm a twenty-nine-year-old single man who owns a garage and works more hours than the sun sees the sky. I'm the uncle who dropped by mostly on occasions that required gifts or turkey with bear hugs, candy, and gentle teasing before dipping again. I'm not the nurturing fatherly type by any stretch of the imagination. And I'm damn sure not equipped to handle a still-grieving, acting-out preteen.

And most of the time, Rose agrees.

Loudly.

This last year has been an emotional roller coaster of anger, pain, sorrow, helplessness, and frustration. For both of us. And every day since my sister's lawyer informed me that I would be responsible for making sure Rose grew into a responsible, well-adjusted, and contributing member of society, I've asked myself

"What the fuck was Mona thinking?" at least twice a day.

And I'd ante up my prized, autographed Russell Wilson Seahawks jersey that Mrs. Reyes poses that very question to herself each time she has to call me down to her office.

"Mr. Hunt, this is Mrs. Reyes, the principal at the elementary school." The principal's cool-under-pressure voice that must be a prerequisite for her profession echoes in my ear. She greets me as if we aren't old acquaintances by now. Hell, if she came to my shop, she'd probably qualify for the friends-'n'-family discount. "There's been an incident with Rose. Could you please come to the school as soon as possible for a conference?"

God no. "Yes." I scrub a rough hand down my face. "I'll be there shortly."

"Thank you, Mr. Hunt."

I end the call and shove my cell back in my front pocket, blowing a hard breath.

"Everything okay, Ace?" my friend and employee Jake Donavan asks, rolling out from underneath a '70 Chevy Nova. That's what Hunt Auto is known for—restoring older cars, as well as the usual tune-ups, alignments, and engine work. And Jake is one of the best. He's also been with me the longest, as he was here when my uncle owned the place. Though several years older than me, we became good friends after my second year in college ended in a spectacular blaze of glory with an obliterated ACL and the termination of my football career. So he knows almost everything that's gone down in my life in the last ten years. One look at my face and a wry, sad smile twists his mouth. "Rose?"

Yeah, he knows only one person is capable of

putting this particular look of "Jesus Christ, what now?" on my face.

"I have to head to the school," I reply, snatching a rag out of my back pocket and wiping my hands. I'll wash them before I go, too, but by now the shit is probably part of my DNA. "Can you take over here for about an hour?"

He nods his head toward the lobby and the entrance. "I got you."

"Thanks," I mutter.

Twenty minutes later, I walk into the elementary school's front office. The administrative assistant, a pretty woman in her mid-twenties with beautiful, long dreads and shaved sides, grins at me, her hazel eyes bright behind her blue-rimmed glasses.

"Hi, Mr. Hunt. How're you doing today?" she greets. All that perkiness has the skin between my shoulder blades itching.

I grunt, glancing at the closed door bearing the "Principal" gold plate. "Been better."

"Well," she gathers a pile of folders and taps them on the wide desk before sliding them in a metal rack, "adult quokkas toss their babies at predators so they can escape. So chin up. Compared to them, you're parenting isn't that bad." She gives me two thumbs-up.

I blink. Stare at her. Blink again. I'm caught somewhere between appalled and... relieved.

Before I can reply, she flicks a hand toward the principal's closed door. "Mrs. Reyes sends her apologizes, but she was unexpectedly called down to the board. So you're going to be meeting with our assistant principal today. Rose is already in there with her."

"That's fine," I say, just as the door next to the principal's opens.

Turning, I brace myself for the next hour and take a step forward. And freeze.

My breath stalls, then stutters in my lungs as my mind completely blanks. Shock seizes my body in a vice grip, locking me down so hard, I'd wince if I could move. The blood in my veins ices over, and if I could breathe, I'm sure it would be white puffs of cold.

But my heart... my heart pounds against my chest, striking it so hard black-and-blue bruises should mottle my skin.

It can't be. I haven't seen her in two years since she fled my house in the middle of the night, her lips swollen from my kiss. No, it's not possible...

"India."

2

India

I'd convinced myself I was prepared for this moment when it inevitably arrived. Told myself that I could not only handle it, but I wouldn't be moved by it. Two years was a long time, and I'd used them to get over the man I'd loved and given my fidelity and heart to for four years. I'd used them to assure myself that kissing his best friend had been an aberration, an emotional blip due to stress, hurt, and the shock and anger at finding out Jessie had betrayed me.

But standing here, meeting Asa Hunt's piercing dove-gray gaze, I could admit I'd been overconfident and a fool. All the internal pep talks and "I am not the same broken woman" mantras in the world couldn't have equipped me for finally facing the man who'd haunted my dreams like a stubborn-ass ghost with an attitude problem.

It didn't seem possible, but he appeared larger than he had when he'd only been Jessie's best friend, and not the man who'd reshaped the definition of a kiss for me. A mechanic, he'd always been muscular, but now, with his long-sleeved black Henley clinging to his powerful shoulders and bulging arms for dear life, it was as if those muscles had spawned offspring. Well over six feet, his sheer height and width seemed to shrink the spacious office to the size of a cubbyhole.

A wide, deep chest. A flat abdomen that I'd bet my Happy Planner boasted a ladder of taut ridges. A tapered waist leading to lean hips that his faded jeans settled on with the help of a dark brown leather belt. Solid thighs whose thickness rivaled the trunks of the soaring oaks outside of the school building.

"India."

My name in that whiskey-poured-over-gravel voice sends a shiver through my body as it drags my gaze back to his. And I immediately want to look anywhere but at that craggy but stunning face of angles, slants, and dips. His broad forehead, sharp cheekbones, lean cheeks, elegant slope of a nose, hard as flint jaw, and wide, criminally full and sensual mouth, framed by a brownish-red scruff.

God, that mouth.

I know the texture of it, the ratio of soft and hard, the intoxicating taste of it. Like dark chocolate dipped in the finest, most expensive brandy. Sweet, strong, and burning.

It's been two years, but there are times when I can still feel the brand of his lips on mine. The delicious tingle his demanding, ravenous kiss left behind...

No. I give myself a rough mental shake. I'm not doing this. I'm not falling down this particular rabbit hole where nothing but hurt, rejection, and confusion await me at the bottom. I decided two years ago never to give myself to another man who doesn't want me—and only me—as much as I want him. And even if I lost my ever lovin' mind and fell for Asa Hunt, it would be a one-way, first-class ticket to heartbreak and disappointment. Other than that night, he'd never exhibited the slightest interest in me. Hell, there were times I questioned Jessie if his best friend even *liked* me.

And there was the other reason Asa was a no-fly zone. In a choice between me and Jessie—well, there wasn't a choice. That bromance exists up there with Ben and Matt, Seth and James... Beavis and Butthead.

Nothing and no one, especially not a woman, will ever come between them. There's something in their past—something Jessie never shared with me—that binds them together tighter than brothers. Blood brothers. And somehow, I think the term literally applies to them.

Briefly closing my eyes, I gather every scrap of hard-won composure I possess and smile politely at him as if I don't know what his groan tastes like.

"Asa," I say, moving forward with my hand extended toward him. "It's been a long time."

There. I sound professional, cool, and most importantly, unaffected.

He blinks, and the shock slowly ebbs from his eyes. His gaze dips to my hand, his brows arrowing down into a forbidding V. My belly flutters at that frown, but I refuse to lower my arm. We're going to be adults here if it kills us.

Eventually, he raises his arm and clasps my hand in his bigger one. Swamping mine. Callouses roughen his palm, lightly scratching my skin, and before I can shut them down, images flood my mind of those large, long-fingered, and surprisingly elegant hands stroking up the sides of my naked torso, those same callouses scraping my tender skin, leaving heat and shivers in their wake. Of those hands cupping my breasts, completely covering them. Then his wide thumbs sweeping over my nipples, drawing them into tight, this-side-of-painful points.

I snatch my hand back and force myself not to rub the palm down my pencil-skirt-covered thigh. Instead, I nod toward Lena, our administrative assistant.

"I heard Lena tell you about why your meeting is with me instead of Mrs. Reyes. I hope that's okay."

"You?" he asks, still wearing that frown. "She said the assistant principal. I thought that was Mr. York."

"He retired at the end of last year," I explain. "If you'll..." I wave a hand toward my office, not really wanting to have this conversation in front of God and Lena. I really like the woman, but she loves gossip the way I crave Idris Elba—with an insatiable lust.

With a barely there dip of his head, he follows me into my office, and I close the door behind him.

"Hey, Uncle Asa," Rose greets her uncle with her outside voice, popping up from one of the chairs in front of my desk. "Isn't it cool that India's my principal? I guess I forgot to tell you that."

I stifle a sigh. The little girl has two volumes. Loud, and holy-shit-dogs-in-a-five-mile-radius-are-howling. Gone is the sweet-tempered, shy child I remember from the handful of times we met at family barbecues and other get-togethers. And in her place is the boisterous, unruly little girl that has become the terror of the fourth grade.

Yet, I have the softest of spots for her. And not just because she's Asa's niece. My heart breaks for her because I know the grief and pain of losing a parent. We're members of a club that no one in their right mind wants to be a part of.

"Rose," I calmly say, arching an eyebrow as I peer

down at her. "What did we talk about how to address me at school?"

Her grin fades, the corners of her mouth turning down. "I should call you Ms. Roberts," she mutters, hunching her shoulders around her ears.

My heart squeezes even as I continue in a gentle but firm voice. The worst thing I can do is let her get away with anything. Forget the mile. She'll take I-90.

"Yes, and it doesn't mean we're not friends. Why do I need you to call me Ms. Roberts?" I press.

"Because it's a sign of respect." Her cute face screws up into a thoughtful pout. "But when we're not at school, I can call you India, right?"

God, she's adorable. She and her lopsided, dark-red bun. Something tells me it's Asa's handywork.

"Sure," I say, although the odds of us seeing each other outside of this building are nil to ain't-gonna-happen. Not because I don't like her, because I do. But that would mean her uncle would have to be with us. And that's a no-go. "Can you go sit down for me? I need to talk to you and your uncle."

"Sure," she grumbled, dragging her bedazzled, pink high-tops the few feet back to the chair. I'm sure a death row inmate heading toward a date with a needle doesn't look as down-in-the-mouth as she did. "Asa?" I step back, and he takes the hint, brushing past me to enter my office.

His scent—sandalwood, an earthy musk, and the underlying spice of clean, hard-won sweat—infiltrates my nostrils, and I belatedly hold my breath. But all that serves to do is trap his unique fragrance in my nose and capture the flavor of it on my tongue.

Jesus, what is wrong with me? I shouldn't be reacting this way to him. Before that night in his house, I didn't even look at Asa in any way except as Jessie's friend. But after he shoved me away as if hissing snakes had sprung up around my head, I told myself that even though his rejection had stung, I was thankful. That kiss, no matter how hot and raw it'd been, was a mistake. Only scorned, bitter women who snatched off wigs on reality shows went after their ex's best friends. And she refused to be *that* woman. Vengeful. Trifling. Petty.

Clearing my throat, I close the door behind me and circle my desk. Lowering into my chair, I wait until Asa's seated before I begin.

"I hate that we're meeting again under these circumstances," I lie. Because if it'd been up to me, we would have never come face-to-face again. He's a reminder of a past I just want to forget. "But Rose had an incident today with another girl in her class."

"An incident," Asa repeats, throwing his niece a narrowed glance.

"Yes, Rose smacked her in the face."

"Dammit, Rose," Asa growls, aiming a fierce scowl down at the little girl. "I thought we talked about this fighting."

"Wasn't much of a fight," Rose mumbled, crossing her arms over her chest and sinking back against the chair. "After I smacked her in the mouth, she started crying and ran to Ms. Hesche." She huffed out a breath, her own scowl darkening her brow. "Tattletale."

"Are you kidding me right now?" Asa snapped, shaking his head. "Rose—"

"No," she fairly shouted, her high-pitched voice ringing in the office. Red poured into her round cheeks and her gray eyes, identical to her uncle's, glistened with tears. "You don't understand, Uncle Asa. Jennifer was making fun of me. I told her to stop. But she kept laughing and telling everyone that Mom died on purpose so she wouldn't have to be my mother anymore." A sob ripped free of her thin, little chest, and those tears rolled down her face. "So I hit her to make her shut up. Because it's not true. It's not true!"

Oh God. My arms ache to wrap themselves around Rose and hold her. To somehow take away the pain that saturates her voice and throbs in each cry.

Jennifer Piece had claimed Rose had hauled off and slapped her for no reason. Not that I believed that bit of nonsense. I'd only been with this school for a couple of months, but I already had that girl's number. She's pretty, with dimples deep enough you just wanted to dip your finger in... and would give the meanest mean girl an inferiority complex.

I hate to say it, but that kid is a bitch on training wheels.

"Of course it's not true, sweet pea," Asa murmurs, cupping the side of his niece's head and pressing his lips to the auburn curls that have escaped her top bun. "It's bullshit and cruel, but Rose," he leans back and waits until she tips her head back to look at him, "you can't go around slapping people. No matter how much they deserve it," he adds on a rumble.

"But—"

"No buts." He shakes his head, and the ends of his auburn-brown hair graze his chin. "You hand over all your power to her when you lose control like that. Now you're in trouble, and she isn't. Even though that doesn't seem fair, either," he says, lifting his head and pinning me with a flinty stare.

I arch an eyebrow. "Oh believe me, we're going to address the other student's actions." At least *I* would be. I hadn't known the exact details of the exchange, since all Rose had said up until now was that Jennifer deserved it. But I don't condone or put up with bullying. She'll be dealt with. "Not that I'm excusing what the other girl said, because it's inexcusable, but the fact is, Rose escalated it by physically hitting her. The school has a no-tolerance policy for violence, so we can't let it go."

"Does the school have a no-tolerance policy against bullying?" he growls. "What kind of kid goes around tormenting someone who just lost her mother? I want to meet her parents so I can tell them what I think about their daughter and them, if they're teaching her to be an overall shitty person."

"Asa," I murmur, leaning forward and flattening my hand on top of my desk. It's the closest I'll allow myself to come to covering his hand. "I agree this is a case of bullying, and I will talk to the child involved, her parents, Rose's teacher, and the other children in the classroom. I won't let it go. I promise."

After a moment, he jerks his head in a sharp nod.

"Now, about Rose." I lean back in my chair, dropping both hands to the arms. "Like I said, the policy is clear on the consequences for physical altercations. So Rose will have to attend in-school suspension for a week. Her teacher will prepare her schoolwork so she won't fall behind in class. But because it is a suspension, she can't ride the bus to and from school." I switch my attention from Asa and his unwavering, intense gaze to the little girl huddled in the chair next to him. "Rose?" I wait until she lifts her chin from her chest and meets my eyes. "I'm very sorry for what was said to you. I remember your mom, and she loved you more than anything. And though we weren't very well acquainted, there's one thing I know for certain. If she could be here with you, she would. There's no truth at all in what Jennifer said."

Her little chin lost some of its stubborn edge, and it wobbled as she sniffed and nodded. "She lies a lot anyway," she whispered, voice hoarse from her tears. "Michael Taylor said she's a bitch, and I think he's right."

"Rose," Asa hissed.

"What?" She blinked up at him. "You say that all the time."

And more, I silently add. Hell, he's said a few of them since we've been sitting in the office.

"Be that as it may," I intervene, throwing Asa a "she's not wrong" look, "we don't say those words in school, and you know that."

"Okay. I'm sorry," she grumbles. Then a couple of seconds later, "But she is."

Since I pretty much agree with her, I decide to let that go, counting her apology as a win.

"You'll have to take Rose home for the rest of the day, and since it's Friday, she'll start the suspension Monday morning." I rise from my chair, ending the meeting. "Have a good weekend, Rose."

She shoves herself out of the chair and turns wide, glistening eyes on me that would've made Puss in Boots look like a rank amateur. "He's going to ground me." She jerks a thumb over her shoulder in the direction of her uncle.

"You got that right." Asa frowns down at her, even as he lays a gentle hand on the back of her head. "Do me a favor. Go outside and sit down in the office. I need to speak to Ms. Roberts for a minute. And Rose," he says, when she trudges past him, "don't move from that chair."

"Yes, Uncle Asa."

He walks over to the door and doesn't close it until her butt hits the chair right outside my office. But when he does shut it, my stomach bottoms out, panic clawing at me like a wild thing. Perspiration springs under my arms and on my palms, and I so desperately want to rub them together, but I refuse to reveal any kind of weakness to that hooded, silver gaze. I'll be damned if he even suspects that he affects me.

Because, dammit, he does affect me.

I want to slap the shit out of my heart for pounding against my rib cage just because that big body is ambling back toward me with that loose, unconsciously sexual gait. A man that large should lumber, plod, lurch. Instead, he... *stalks*. And my heart and vagina approve.

Traitorous bitches. Both of them.

Asa stops in front of my desk, staring at me. And I stare right back.

At the dark auburn waves that glance his cheekbones and caress his jaw. At the scruff that's about an hour past a five o'clock shadow. At the tattoos crawling up his neck and down his wrists from under the cuffs of his shirt. At the perfection of his mouth that carries this almost cruel slant, but I know for a fact can be gentle as well as bruising.

Oh, I stare. Because I couldn't tear my gaze away from him if Jesus Christ Himself rode down here with a train of cherubim in His wake declaring, *Have thou some damn dignity*.

"Was there something else you needed to discuss with me about Rose?" I finally ask.

"Where've you been?"

The blunt demand doesn't brook anything but obedience, an answer. That angers me. And damn, it excites me. That tone brings to mind how those huge hands gripped me down on his lap, held me still to take the roll and thrust of his dick over my jeans-covered clit, clasped my head and fucked my mouth like it was my pussy.

Heat, hot and throbbing, echoes between my legs like a tiny heartbeat, and my nipples tighten under my bra. I *ache*. Thank God for the suit jacket I didn't take off when he arrived. It's my only saving grace, sparing me from utter humiliation.

"Where I've been has nothing to do with Rose," I say, impressed that my voice is all *I'm a professional*, instead of *None of your fucking business*. "Now if you have any questions about the suspension or would like to set up a meeting with her guidance counselor—"

"Where. Have. You. Been?" A muscle ticks along his jaw, and it's a flashing warning sign that his patience is running out.

"My. Business."

He's part of my past, and I never invited him into my present or my future. Besides, he has zero right to ask me that question. He's Jessie's friend; he was never mine. We just lip-locked for one crazy-ass moment in time.

That muscle jumps harder, faster, and his mouth almost flattens into a grim line. *Almost*, because curves that full could never completely thin out.

"Do you know how fucking worried I was when you ran out of the house that night?" The low, rumbling thunder in his voice vibrates right through me. It's that kind of threatening thunder that heralds one hell of a storm. He slaps his palms down on the desktop and leans forward, his large frame nearly stretching across the width of the piece of furniture. His eyes are molten with barely concealed anger, his dark brows arrowing down over them. "I tried calling to make sure you were okay, and you didn't answer. I went by your house the next damn day, but you'd cleared out. No trace of you, India. It was like you vanished off the face of the damn earth. So where in *the fuck* have you been?"

"Why would you come looking for me?" Bewildered and more than a little shocked, I search his face with its strong bones and elegant slopes. Meet his narrowed glare. "Why did you care?"

Anger rolls off of him like sinuous, steamy waves off a sidewalk. Since he walked into my office, he somehow managed to keep this rage under wraps, but now, with his niece out of room, he unleashes it.

"Are you shitting me right now?" he snaps.

But no. I'm really not. I really don't understand why he cared. I was his best friend's ex. A woman he kissed and immediately regretted doing so. I thought now, as I did then, that he was relieved to be rid of me. I started that whole inappropriate snowball rolling.

I cried on his chest.

I climbed on his lap.

I kissed him first.

So yes, I'm confused. Sue me.

"You were hurt, confused, and in pain. Of course I cared. You were my best friend's—"

"Girlfriend," I finish for him, when he bites off the rest of the sentence. "I was Jessie's girlfriend, and we kissed. And then, you could barely look at me. Of course, that was after you pushed me off you like I had suddenly contracted a contagious disease. Like I disgusted you."

My softly spoken words plummet between us like a verbal bomb, and the reverberations bounce off the walls, seeming to gain speed and volume with each pass.

There.

It's out now.

No ignoring it no matter how much he might have preferred to. We both preferred to.

"You didn't disgust me." He slowly straightens, his arms crossing over his massive chest. "You could never... *Fuck*," he growls, dragging a hand through his hair and fisting the strands at the crown before releasing them. "Where have you been?" he demands again.

I almost beg him to finish what he started. I want to know what would've come next. But I stopped being a masochist two years ago.

"Seattle." A dull ache throbs in my temples, and I need this done, over with. And if that means giving him the information he wants so he can leave my office, then I'm willing to concede this battle. "I lived with a friend from college, taught at a school there and earned my EDS in leadership. When the position for assistant principal opened here, I applied. End of story."

Except, *not* end of story. The explanation didn't include the nights I spent on my friend's plaid, worn couch, staring dry-eyed at the water-marked, popcorn ceiling because I'd cried so much my tear ducts were in a drought. Or how anger, grief, and guilt had moved in my chest like squatters who refused to be evicted. Or how for several months I'd gone on total self-destruct and became a serial one-night-stander who fucked random guys just to prove to myself that I was desirable, sexy... wanted.

Thank God that phase didn't last long. Letting a man treat my body like his personal playground had not only been stupid as fuck, but it hadn't affirmed me. It'd just made me feel cheap, used. Not knocking the women who indulge in and enjoy casual sex—I'm not shaming them, and hell, more power to them. But

I'm not that woman. I was punishing myself for not being enough for Jessie.

And that was utter bullshit. Jessie cheating had to do with his character, loyalty, and heart. Not mine. Definitely not my worth.

It'd taken time, plenty of Come-to-Jesus talks, and lots of hours of Dr. Phil to come to that realization.

But I'm not sharing any of that with Asa. We're not bosom buddies, and I don't want or need his pity or judgement.

"Does Jessie know you're back?"

His question ricochets through me, momentarily knocking me off balance. Not because I still have feelings for Jessie. Thanks to the men my mother dated, I had a front row seat to what cheating does to a woman. How it breaks her heart, demeans her, whittles away her self-esteem. That's always been a deal breaker for me. Something Jessie knew. So, no. I'm over him.

Still, the thought of confronting my past after I ran from it for two years... It has a pang of fear ringing inside me.

"No," I say, harsher than I intended. "Why would he?"

Asa is silent, just studies me with those eyes that have always been too sharp, too incisive... just "too." Even when I'd been his best friend's woman, that gaze had been both beautiful and a weight. One I'd wanted to analyze like one of my textbooks, and dodge like a child caught doing something naughty.

And didn't that just sum up my every interaction with him.

"I'll have to tell him." He briefly glances away from me and out the window on the far wall of my office. "I can't let him be blindsided."

"Of course not." I'm unable to keep my mouth from twisting into a bitter smile. "I expected nothing less of his ever loyal, devoted best friend."

His head snaps back toward me. Though his face remains as stoic as ever, hurt flashes in his eyes before it, too, disappears behind shutters. My breath snares in my throat, snagging on the regret that immediately pierces me like razor-tipped thorns.

"We both know I'm not that loyal." He pauses. "Or honest."

If I'd harbored the slightest confusion about what he meant, his gaze dropping to my mouth would've cleared it up in a hurry.

Jesus. I freeze, but an inferno incinerates me from the inside out. Last time he looked at me like this, his tongue ended up in my mouth, making a mockery of every kiss I'd experienced until that moment. And I'd ended up damn near coming on his cock with layers of denim and cotton separating us. Just from his lips and a couple of strokes over my clit.

I should tell him to stop it. Tell him that he doesn't have the right to stare at me like that. Like he wants me, when we both know he doesn't.

Instead, I slick the tip of my tongue over my suddenly dry lips.

Smolder. That's what his eyes do. They *smolder*. And I'm seared by that hooded inspection.

Oh God. I'm going to do something monumentally foolish and beg him to extinguish the fire he's stoked inside me. To do it with those large, graceful hands. With his wicked tongue. With that powerful body.

With his big cock.

I shiver, and from the quicksilver flicker in those gray depths, he catches it. His full lips part, and I swear I hear his coarse rasp of air. And it brushes over my skin, scrapes over my nipples. Grazes my lower belly. Caresses my clit and already wet flesh.

My desk phone buzzes, and Lena's voice echoes through the intercom. "Ms. Roberts, Mrs. Reyes is on line one for you."

I press the reply button and silently thank the patron saint of timely interruptions. "Thanks, Lena." Releasing the button, I return my attention to Asa and fix what I hope is a polite but distant smile on my face. "I have a call, Asa. Thanks for coming in to talk about Rose. And like I said, I promise to follow up on the other student."

"India—"

"No." I slam up a hand, palm out. "Not here and not now." Not ever, if I have my way. "Please... just let it go."

For a moment, he frowns, and his eyes darken, reminding me of a sky just before a storm hits. But then, his expression clears, and it's that indecipherable mask again. Relief and frustration burrow through me, but when he turns and stalks toward the door, I don't stop him.

And when he disappears into the outer office, I try to convince myself it's for the best.

I almost succeed.

Almost.

Shaking my head, I reach for the phone receiver, but pause as the button for line one remains dim instead of lit up. Just as I hit the intercom button, Lena pokes her head around my doorway.

"Hey, you're welcome for that diversion." She strolls in and flops down in the chair Asa vacated. "I gave myself ten minutes before sending the date-from-hell save." She arches an eyebrow. "Not that I would ever want to be saved from that guy. Rawr." She paws the air.

Even as I stare at her and her pseudo cat claws in mingled shock and horror, a laugh surges up my throat. Settling for a snicker so I don't encourage her too much, I roll my eyes and sink back down into my desk chair.

"And how do you know I needed to be rescued?"

"C'mon, India," she scoffs, using my first name as opposed to the more formal Ms. Roberts. She addresses me casually when kids and parents aren't around. "The way that man stared at you? I was going to throw either condoms or life jackets in there. And since your face had more of a Jack-sinking-into-icy-depths than a I-wanna-smash-that look, I went with the save." Hazel eyes gleaming behind her retro glasses, she digs into the small bowl of peanut M&Ms on my desk. "So dish. What's the deal between you two?"

Sighing, I fall back against the chair, tired. "It's a long, complicated story."

She pops a brown M&M in her mouth and chews, silently contemplating me. "Ben didn't come home last night, and when I woke up this morning, there was a Dear John letter waiting for me on the dining room table. Apparently, I'm an ambition succubus, and my lack of motivation in settling for being a school secretary instead of pursuing a "real" career is bumming him out. So he's taken off for Alaska to fulfill his life-long dream." She pauses, and I can't lie. I'm hanging on every. Fucking. Word. "Crab fishing in the Bering Sea. It seems Ben's life-long dream is being an extra on *Deadliest Catch*."

"Holy. Shit." I whisper, stunned. No, flabbergasted.

Her boyfriend of five years left her for a goddamn snow crab.

"Yep." She tosses another piece of candy into her mouth and crunches loudly.

"Oh, Lena." She might be flippant about the abrupt ending of her relationship, but now I glimpse the pain she's managed to keep under wraps all day. "This calls for wine."

"Yes. Wine and a mutual sharing of war stories. Friends don't let friends share all their humiliating shit without serving up their own so they have blackmail ammo on each other. It's just not done. Bad form, Roberts."

"Fine." I laugh, even though my chest is aching for her. "After we get out of here, we head straight to the store to pick up alcohol, pizza, chips, and ice cream. Because friends also don't let friends become a drunk, blubbering mess in public."

"Deal." Lean grins and pushes up out of the chair and with a finger crinkle, exits.

Damn.

Men are such assholes.

3

India

Early Monday afternoon, I poke my head into the classroom set aside for in-school detention. It's lunch time, and the teacher, Mr. Keiser, sits at his desk, unwrapping his sandwich. He glances up at me, and I wave before shifting my attention to Rose, who occupies one of the thirty chair-desk combos at the far side of the room. She's the only student here this week —so far. Sometimes it's just one or two kids in here, and other days, the room's almost filled to capacity. It's like their behavior is dictated by the moon or Mercury in retrograde.

"Hi, Mr. Keiser." I step inside the classroom. "If you'd like a break, I can cover for you. I'll stay here with Rose."

He shrugs, gathering up his lunch. "Thanks for the offer. I'll be back by the end of the lunch period."

"Sounds good." I smile, and as soon as the door closes behind him, I make my way through the desks until I reach Rose's. She watches me, her elfin face screwed up in a suspicious frown.

God, she's adorable. With her beautiful and unruly auburn curls, several shades lighter than her uncle's—today pulled into a slightly misshapen side braid—gray eyes, small bow of a mouth, and delicate features, she's a pretty girl who will grow into a truly stunning woman. Her mom had been beautiful, too. I'd witnessed a man literally stumble over his feet and get gut-punched by a table in a bar we all hung out at one night a few years ago.

God, Mona. I'm so sorry that you had to let this lovely girl go so soon.

The words whisper through my head and heart. And though I'm not a particularly spiritual person, I hope they reach Mona wherever she is.

"You look so much like your mom," I say to Rose, turning the desk in front of her around to face her before sliding into it.

I shift my focus to removing my container from my lunch bag and removing the lid over my salad. Better that than lose myself in the mixture of sorrow and eagerness that fill this little girl's dove-gray eyes. Because if I lose myself in that emotion, I'll be in danger of picking this girl up and hugging her close until those chunks of pain and grief start to break up and loosen.

When I have my emotions under control, I look at her again and smile.

"That's what Grammy says. And Uncle Asa, too. But I think they just tell me that to make me feel better." She picks up a half of her sandwich and starts peeling off the crust. "They don't like to talk about Mom a lot. Even though I want to. But it makes them sad. So I don't."

Oh God, she's breaking my heart.

"I think you're right. Talking about your mom

probably does hurt them," I agree, my voice a little thick. Both from her loss, her family's and even mine. "She was their daughter and sister, and they miss her a lot. But I bet if you told them how you felt, that talking about your mom makes you feel better, they would gladly listen to everything you want to say. And even add their own memories, because they have a ton."

"You think so?" she asks, and the tentative hope in her voice steals another piece of my heart. And that piece has her name on it.

"I *know* so, Rose." Since I can't hug her, I settle for gently covering her hand and squeezing.

She nods and takes a bite out of her crustless sandwich. After a moment of silent chewing, she tilts her head to the side, studying me with the guileless curiosity and dash of suspicion that children have down to an art form.

"How come you know so much about dead moms?" she challenged.

How do you know so much... The correction hovers on my tongue, and it requires every ounce of restraint not to correct the bald question. I'm a teacher. Sue me.

"Because I lost mine, too." Her mouth forms a small "o." I clear my throat and fork some salad into my mouth, chewing and swallowing before continuing. "I was a little older than you, but she had a bad disease. Cancer."

Rose nods, the slightly frizzy curls catching the sunlight filtering through the window blinds. "My grammy's sister, Aunt Billie, had cancer, too. She had her boobies cut off."

I cough, spinach leaves lodging in my throat. Quickly, I reach for the bottle of water in my bag and twist the cap off. Downing a large gulp, I free the salad from my windpipe.

Jesus Christ.

"You okay?" Rose inquires, frowning. She reaches over and pats my hand. "You probably should've chewed your food more instead of just swallowing. That's what my grammy tells me."

"I'm fine. Thanks." Taking one last sip, I set the bottle down and cross my arms on top of the desk. "Uh, Rose, where did you hear about your, um, aunt?"

"My grammy told my mom about it. I was in my room, but I heard them talking."

Oh boy. "It sounds like your Aunt Billie had breast cancer. Just like my mom. Do you know what cells are?" Rose shakes her head. "They're like really tiny Legos, and they make up our bodies. Sometimes cells don't follow the rules and misbehave. When they do this, they grow into cancer. And when that happens, people can get really sick." I pause, making sure she's with me. When she doesn't interrupt, but just continues to study me, I continue. "So the doctor has to remove the cancer from where it is. I think that's what you probably heard your grandmother describing. So it doesn't necessarily mean her," *Lord, have mercy*, "boob was cut off. It could mean the doctor just took some of it away so she could feel better again." I smile. "But you should really talk to your grandmother about this, okay? She can answer any questions you might have."

After a moment, she nods. "Okay." I release a silent, long, *relieved* breath. Thank God that tough topic was over—

"Is your dad dead, too?"

Good. God.

"No," I reply, judging how do I explain to a ten-year-old that the man called my sperm donor didn't even stick around long enough to find out if he was having a daughter or a junior. "My dad isn't dead. He just wasn't ready to be a father, so it was just my mother and me."

"Ohhh." Again, she nods. Then, "My dad's a deadbeat."

Oh for the love of... "Rose, I'm sure... uh, who told you that?"

"I heard Grammy and Uncle Asa talking about him after Mom died. Uncle Asa was saying we should let my dad know about Mom, and Grammy said she wasn't telling that deadbeat anything."

"Let me guess," I drawled. "You were in your room, but you were listening."

"Unhuh," she agreed.

"Rose, I think these are things you should really talk to your grandmother and uncle about. And it might be a good idea if you stopped eavesdropping," I suggested.

Rose shrugs, totally unrepentant. "How else am I supposed to find out anything?"

"You ask, and then they'll tell you if they don't want to answer. Maybe try that next time?"

"Okay," she mutters, sounding less than thrilled about that option. She attacks the other half of her sandwich, peeling off the crust. After a moment, she tilts her head and treats me to another one of those looks that has me bracing for whatever's going to come out of her mouth. "India, can I ask you a question then?"

We're in school, but I don't correct her. It's just us two here, and this feels more like... family than student teacher.

"Of course."

She hesitates and dips her chin. Even though the crust is gone, she starts tearing into the bread. "Why aren't you sad anymore?" she whispers.

I don't need to ask her to clarify; her meaning is crystal clear to me. That's one of the things about being a member of our special club. We have our own language.

"It isn't that I'm not sad anymore, Rose. I still miss her, and that doesn't go away," I murmur. "Moms are special and deserve to be missed. But I promise you not every day will be a sad one. Soon, when you think of your mom, instead of crying, you'll laugh at something funny she said or you two did together. You know what my mom told me?"

She shakes her head so hard, the tail of her braid brushes her chest, staring at me as if my next words will be as momentous as Moses' pronouncement from the mount. Or Taylor Swift's next tweet.

"She said as long as I have my memories of us together, she will always be with me. So, Rose," I reach forward, smooth a hand down her slightly crooked braid, and tug on the end, "You'll never be alone because your mom is with you as long as you keep her here." I cover my heart. "And here." Then tap my temple.

Rose nods, her big gray eyes glistening with tears and her bottom lip trembling before she sank her teeth into it.

"Okay then—*oof!*"

Thin, fragile arms circle my neck and squeeze so hard they momentarily cut off my breath. And I'm okay with that. As her small body trembles and her tears dampen my shirt collar, I'm okay with that.

∽

"You want to explain why my niece is suddenly asking her grandmother and me about mastectomies, deadbeats, and heaven?"

I whip around, jerking my attention away from the car line and the last few parents picking up their kids to the growling, frowning giant behind me.

Dammit, he shouldn't look so freaking... good. Yes, I'm a college graduate with a bachelor's and master's, and this is what he's reduced me to. *Good*.

The man wears a scowl like it's a fashion statement, and *God*, he's doing for it what an Armani suit does for a model. Those heavy, dark brows drawn tightly together emphasize the beauty of his silver gaze and the autocratic arrogance of his nose. The pulled-down corners of his mouth only accentuate the wicked, erotic fullness of his lips. The clench of his jaw draws my eyes to the forbidding strength of it.

I want to yell, "For godsakes, man, smile!" But witnessing that sinful mouth curved in pleasure and those eyes bright with delight would be even more devastating to my respiratory and reproduction systems. And I've just started here at the elementary school. I can't show up asthmatic and spontaneously pregnant.

Aaaaand I'm mentally babbling to myself. Jesus Christ.

"What are you doing here?" I demand. Seriously. My school should be a safe space.

"Picking up my niece," he says. The "*for real?*" isn't vocalized, but it's heard.

It's official. He's killing my brain cells.

"Right." I turn back around and resume monitoring the thinning after-school traffic. Bringing my walkie-talkie up, I press the button on the side. "Erin,"

I call to the teacher in charge of watching over the car-riders in the gym, "could you send someone to get Rose Hunt from the in-school suspension classroom? Her uncle's here to pick her up." Glancing over my shoulder, I throw Asa a bland smile. "She should be out shortly."

"Okay, thanks. Now answer my question." He shifts forward, and his broad shoulders fill my view along with the ever-present frown. "Rose told us she spoke with you yesterday about cancer, her father and mother. You don't think that's something you should've called me about? I'm her uncle and guardian. You're her assistant principal, not her family. It wasn't your place to have that conversation with her."

Anger, and yes, dammit, *hurt* swirls in my stomach, then surges up my chest and throat in a scalding flood. Just before the caustic stream can pour off my tongue, I clamp my teeth together. And breathe. Breathe past the fury, the solid punch to my feelings.

Rose. This is about Rose.

The mantra marches through my mind on a desperate campaign to keep my control tightly leashed.

Turning, I wave at the teacher assisting me this afternoon. "Would you mind taking over for a couple of minutes?"

"Of course." She pops up her thumb. "I got this."

I smile at her, but it disappears from my mouth like Houdini when I face Asa again. "Please follow me."

Not waiting for his agreement, I pivot and stride toward the other end of the platform where no students or parents linger. He's right behind me, and when I face him again, the air damn near vibrates with the tension arcing between us.

"One, you're correct and I'm sorry," I grind out.

Surprise flashes through his eyes at my apology, but that only pricks my anger more. As if he's shocked that I would or could admit to being wrong. I always suspected Asa didn't think very highly of me. Even when I was with Jessie, he seemed stand-offish. Reticent. Several times it occurred to me that he only put up with being around me because I was with his best friend. Which was why that kiss shook me to my core. Left me reeling with confusion and aching with hunger. I felt humiliated, played. Used. He turned me into a fucking cliché, the "good girl" panting after the bad boy.

I've never forgiven him or myself for that night.

Though Jessie had betrayed me, I nearly mauled his friend hours later without officially breaking up with him. And I enjoyed it. God, I lost myself in his mouth, his hands, his body. Maybe I wouldn't have stopped at a kiss if Asa hadn't shoved me off of him.

And that not-knowing haunts me.

That I can still feel the beautiful, dirty pressure of his cock rolling over my pussy torments me.

That I crave it again tortures me.

Inhaling a deep breath, I focus on getting through this confrontation. "You're right. I should've called you after speaking with Rose yesterday, especially given the content of the conversation. That was my responsibility to you as her guardian."

He stared at me, his gaze roaming over my face. "Thank you for that. I appreciate it."

"Yes, well, don't thank me just yet," I snap, edging forward into his space, fury dancing just under my skin. "I was wrong, but you are, too. I was with Jessie for four years, which means you and your family were also in my life for four years. I might not have been close with Mona, but I knew her. I talked with her. Laughed with her. Broke bread with her. The same with Rose. So maybe I'm not *family*, but I'm more than just her assistant principal. I'm her friend."

"India..." he murmurs.

"No," I interrupt him, emotion bubbling fast and furious inside me. A part of me whispers that my reaction is a little disproportionate to his accusation. But I call *bullshit* on that part. It's been two years of pent-up frustration, anger, and hurt, and like a bubbling pot left unattended, I'm boiling over. "Rose has questions about her mother—ones she didn't feel comfortable going to you and your mom about, because she didn't want to cause you any more pain by talking about Mona. Since I lost my mother, too, I answered those I could, but told her she shouldn't be afraid to speak with you and her grandmother. Especially since she's taken up eavesdropping as her way of getting those answers. So her coming to you yesterday was her way of showing she trusted you. Which you should be delighted with, not jumping on my ass about. Maybe I overstepped a little for an assistant principal, but not a friend. It would've been cruel to leave her hurting, and I wasn't about to do that."

Silence plummets between us. Only our harsh breaths score the air.

The anger shifts, still containing that serrated, fiery edge, but... different.

Hotter. More feral.

Everything else—the high-pitched voices of children, the lower tones of teachers and parents, the rumbles of cars and honks of their horns—fades, swallowed up by the thickness surrounding us.

At over six feet, he towers over me, his broad shoulders blocking out the school behind him, his chest seeming as wide and hard as the brick walls comprising the building. Maybe some women, given the disparity in our sizes, would feel intimidated, overpowered. Not me. I feel surrounded. Covered... protected. Because I have intimate knowledge of how gentle those large hands can be. How his big frame offers shelter, comfort.

How it's built for a woman's pleasure.

I don't dare tempt fate and glance down his torso to the flat, muscular abdomen, the narrow waist, and thick, powerful thighs. With his sandalwood-and-earth scent teasing me, wrapping around me in a musk-filled embrace, taking in the rest of him might be my undoing. So far, I've managed to conceal my rebellious and totally inconvenient desire for him. He rejected me once. No way in hell am I giving him another opportunity to tell me I'm a mistake.

Though my mother loved me enough for two parents, I was still a mistake for her and my absentee father. Then, the man I loved obviously hadn't been emotionally ready to balance a sports career and a committed relationship. I'd ended up being the casualty, his mistake. And when Asa looked at me, all he saw was his betrayal of Jessie.

No, I'm done. The next relationship I enter will be one where I'm valued, loved, and accepted.

There's only so much punishment I can inflict on myself.

"I'm sorry." The low, velvet-and-gravel rumble of his apology strokes over me, like fingertips dragging down skin. Caressing me. Marking me. "And thank you."

I blink. Now it's my turn to be surprised. Hell, *shocked*. It's not the first apology he's given me. But it's the first one coupled with gratitude. The first one directed *toward* me but not *about* me.

"You're welcome," I whisper.

Another silence falls over us, and I can't stop looking into those beautiful eyes. And when his gaze dips to my mouth, I can't stop thinking how I want him to take it again. Own it again.

Fuck it again.

"Uncle Asa!"

We both jerk hard, stumbling away a couple of steps as Rose's voice reaches us seconds before she launches her petite body at Asa. She does it with all the exuberance and trust of someone who knows she will be caught. And he does catch her. Asa's arms wrap around her, swinging her up for a big hug before lowering her back to the ground.

A pang of envy reverberates in my chest, and I'm disgusted by it, by me. Yet, I can't deny that I've never had that kind of complete faith in someone other than my mother. Even with Jessie. As much as I'd loved him, he hadn't been my soft place to land. Maybe because I'd lost the one person who'd been that for me... Maybe because of his career that took him away from me so often... Maybe because I'd just been scared... Whatever the reason, I hadn't fully trusted him with the confidence and utter abandon that Rose displayed.

Did Jessie sense that? Was that part of the reason he cheated? Because I didn't give him all of me?

The questions blasted through my mind in rapid-fire succession. A part of me automatically rebelled, yelling a firm, "*Hell no.*" But the other half...

"Hey." Asa's rumbled murmur yanks me from my spiraling free-fall of self-introspection. He studies me through slightly narrowed eyes. "You okay?"

Forcing a smile, I shake off the unnerving thought

that maybe I'm not as healed as I believed. "Of course," I reply, and switch my attention to Rose and away from that too-perceptive-for-my-comfort gaze. "How was your day, Rose?"

Her face pulls into a moue of profound disgust that only little girls can manage. "Booooring. I'm never going back to in-school 'spension again. Or at least not by myself. I think it'd be more fun if I had a friend with me," she adds with a decisive nod.

I lock my jaw so the bark of laughter pressing at my throat doesn't escape. I mean, technically, she's not *wrong*...

"I think you're missing the point of in-school suspension," Asa drawls, tugging on her puffy ponytail. "It's not supposed to be fun. So how about we just go ahead with never going back?"

"Okay," she mumbles. But in the next instant, her face brightened, and she tipped her head back to beam up at her uncle. "It's Pizza Night! And it's my turn to pick what goes on it!"

"That's right." Is it my imagination or did he just pale a little? "But remember, last time it was your turn we agreed anchovies and pineapple don't go together."

Ohhh. That explains the queasy expression.

This time I don't smother my snicker.

Asa arches an eyebrow. "I don't care. Go 'head and judge. That shit was worse than the time Jessie decided to try out his mother's meatloaf recipe."

I recoil, instinctively splaying my fingers over my lurching stomach, the memory of that culinary tragedy still having the power to make me cringe after all these years. Jessie had decided to add ingredients to his mom's already perfect meatloaf to give it some "pizazz." Ketchup is pizazz. Not ketchup, relish, mustard, sauerkraut, horseradish and mozzarella cheese.

As the good girlfriend, I'd eaten it. Not that it'd stayed down long.

"God, no," I object. "Nothing is as bad as that mess. Chemical waste served up with a side of anthrax isn't as bad as that meatloaf."

"Then I suggest you don't order a large pizza with pineapple, onions, goat cheese, and extra anchovies." He shudders, his thick lashes sweeping down to briefly conceal his eyes. "Promise you, I learned my lesson. That's the last time I ever tell her she can order whatever she wants."

"It looked so pretty though," Rose pipes up, grinning. "Uncle Asa says he now has veto power. India—I mean, Ms. Roberts! Why can't you come over for Pizza Night?" Before giving me the chance to turn down the offer, she swings her attention back to Asa. "Please? Can she come for Pizza Night?" Her gaze ricochets back to me. "I'll even order what you want and won't complain. Well, I won't say it to you. Pleeeaaase."

Well shit.

Those wide gray eyes are unfair and sneaky weapons of mass destruction. As is the wheedling note in her voice. But, as much as I hate to disappoint her, I can't. Spend an evening with Asa? We can't even get along on school grounds with plenty of witnesses around us. Being alone with him? Yeah, no.

Besides, when I returned here, one of my resolutions was to keep my distance from everything and everyone in my past. Start as fresh as possible without any baggage. Asa is the very definition of baggage.

"Rose, thank you for the invitation. But I'm sure your uncle was looking forward to just the two of you—"

"I don't mind," Asa interrupts my excuse.

I blink, gaping at him. Surely he didn't... I gave the

man an easy out, for God's sake. What the hell was he thinking? He doesn't like me. Had basically just chewed me out over getting too personal with his niece. Now he wants me to join them for a night of pizza? Yes, he apologized, but still... Except for a kiss he immediately regretted, the man has never liked me. Has always treated me like I was patient zero for Ebola.

"See?" Rose jumps all over Asa's agreement and, releasing her hold on him, throws herself at me. She wraps her arms around my waist, and it's such a sweet, innocent embrace, I don't even have the heart to admonish her about us still being on school grounds. Not with glee lighting her eyes and that huge grin nearly splitting her face in half. "Please? It'll be so much fun. We watch movies, too. And even though I really, *really* want to watch *Moana*, I'll let you pick the movie *and* the pizza."

Damn.

I'm going to cave.

While the thought of returning to Asa's house, the site of The Humiliation, has the soles of my feet itching to break the record for the hundred-yard dash, the possibility of witnessing Rose's eyes dim with disappointment stifles the urge.

I'm trapped into spending the evening with Asa Hunt by an adorable little con artist.

"Okay, then, sure." I try to pour all the enthusiasm I can muster into those three words. "Let's do it."

And as Rose yells her victory, fist pumping and performing an awkward but cute shuffle dance, I can't help but glance at her silent uncle.

His hooded gaze ensnares me, setting my heart into a primal beat against my rib cage.

Dangerous. I'm playing a dangerous game here.

If I had the sense God gave a pet rock, I'd risk upsetting Rose in the name of self-preservation.

But as I agree to meet them at six o'clock, all I can do is hope—*pray*—that I remember the rules this time around. And try my damnedest not to break them.

4

Asa

I freely admit to being a dominant man who likes to be in control. Some would even say I have control issues, which is fair. I'd been the "man" of my house from an early age, with my mother at her job more hours than she'd been at home. Later, when my football dreams ended with a torn ACL and the revocation of my athletic scholarship, I had to take my suddenly altered future and create a new one for myself that didn't include a professional career in the NFL. And then I had to take a quarter-away-from-failing business and transform it into a thriving one.

Yeah, control is important to me.

So how the fuck did I completely lose it on the sidewalk in front of an elementary school? Ever since I drove out of the parking lot with a chattering Rose in the backseat, I've been rewinding and replaying that whole scene, wondering where in the hell it went left. When Rose invited India to our weekly night of pizza and movies, I should've gently but firmly told her *no*. I should've shut that shit down as soon as it popped out of her mouth.

Instead, my tongue flipped my brain the middle finger and backed up Rose's invitation.

And now, hours later, sitting on my couch, watching as Moana restores Te Fiti's heart, I'm in my own personal hell.

India's back in my house. I never thought we would be here again.

And all I can do is remember is the last time she was here. Not that I ever forgot—how could I? That kiss had been better than the best sex I'd ever had. But somehow, with her within these walls, the memories are richer, more vivid. So is the guilt, the shame. Ball-twisting pleasure and dirty shame—I can't separate the two. They're like abusive partners who refuse to leave one another. Yet...

I glance over my shoulder toward the foyer. And in like instant and total recall, my mind provides the image of us sprawled on the same dark laminate flooring, my hands buried in her hair, our mouths eating at one another. I can hear our groans, her soft whimpers, and the soft suction of our tongues and lips meeting, parting, meeting...

Fuck.

I shift on the couch cushion, restless, but forcing myself to focus on Rose's favorite cartoon. Not on her light giggles and India's huskier chuckles. Not on India braiding Rose's curly hair into two neat and cute braids on either side of her head, making my daily attempts look like the amateurish jobs they are. Not on how the sight of her caring for and paying special attention to my niece squeezes my chest so tight my lungs threaten to revolt.

Not on how every smile, every laugh, every teasing remark has me curling my fingers into fists so I don't do something monumentally stupid like reach over and tunnel the afore-mentioned fingers into her gorgeous curls. Not on how her red-and-black plaid shirt stretches across her gorgeous breasts or how the dark, skinny-leg jeans glove her wide, feminine hips and beautiful thick thighs like their only purpose in life is to be next to her skin.

No. Not focusing on any of that at all.

"Can I see yet?" Rose asks, for about the hundredth time since India offered to style her hair. I should've been offended at the quickness that Rose jumped all over that. But hell, I'd seen my handiwork. I can't blame the girl. "Is it done?"

India finishes wrapping a sunflower tie around the end of one of the long braids then squeezes Rose's shoulders. "Go ahead. Let me know what you think. If you don't like it, we can take it out."

Like she'd been propelled from a cannon, Rose shoots to her feet and bolts from the room. Moments later, she charges back in and hurls herself at India. On instinct, I shift, my hands up to catch Rose and steady India. But my precaution isn't needed.

India closes her arms around my niece, hugging her tight, and Rose clings to her, her face buried in India's neck.

"I love it." Rose's words are muffled, but I catch them. And apparently, so does India, since her lashes lower and a spasm of emotion crosses her face. I know that look. Love. Pain. The perfect co-mingling of both. "Thank you so much, India."

"You're so welcome, Rose," she whispers, drawing back so she can smile at my niece. "Anytime. I'll send your uncle some DIY videos so he can learn how to do this."

She slides me a side-eye, and I snort. Yeah, not gonna happen. I can replace a timing belt with no problem, but *that*? I'm failing at Ponytails 101, so the perfectly symmetrical braids aren't looking too good.

"Yeah, he can't do this," says my ten-year-old Judas. "But he's the best at pancakes," she adds, giving me a thumbs up.

I grunt, pushing to my feet, not appeased by the bone she just lobbed at my head. "It's time you got ready for bed, Sweet Pea. Tell India good night, then hit the shower and brush your teeth." I narrow my eyes on her. "And that means don't just let the water run while you do whatever you do in there. Get. In. The. Shower."

"Okay, okay," she mutters. "Thanks for coming over for Pizza Night, India." A big grin transforms her I-don't-want-a-shower frown, and she hugs India once more. "I had so much fun! You need to come again next week."

"We'll see." India tugs on the end of her braid. "Thanks for inviting me. And I'll see you tomorrow at school."

"Okay." She nods, still beaming. "Night!"

Rose disappears down the hall, and a few moments later the bathroom door bangs shut. I sigh. Someday she's going to learn how to quietly shut a door. Someday. I just hope my doorjambs can survive the abuse in the meantime.

"She's wonderful," India murmurs, staring after Rose. Shaking her head, she stands, stretching her arms high over her head and rolling to her toes.

Goddammit.

I rip my too-obsessed gaze away, training it on the oil-stained box of pizza. But I can't unsee the lift of her breasts or that sliver of smooth, chestnut skin as the hem of her shirt rises above her jeans. I can't unhear that low half-moan, half-sigh that escapes her just before she lowers her arms to her sides and her feet back to the floor.

That satisfied-yet-needy sound sizzles down my spine and wraps around my cock in a long, hard, fucking ruthless stroke. It's the cousin to the one she emitted when I rubbed her pussy over my cock. Sweat pops under my arms and fine pricks of sensation dance across my scalp and down the nape of my neck.

"I should be going. Work in the morning," she says from behind me.

I close my eyes, grateful for the reprieve and the excuse to get her out of my house. Having her here... I don't trust myself. Guilt and loyalty aren't enough to keep my thoughts to myself. It won't take much for my hands to cross that line, too.

"Yeah, let me walk you to the door." I pick up the box of pizza, and after a quick detour to the kitchen to dump it, I wait in the living room entryway while she gathers her jacket and purse. "Thanks for hanging tonight. Rose really enjoyed it."

"I did, too." She smiles and it's small, rueful. "I have to confess, I wanted to turn her down. I thought this would be too... awkward. But it turned out okay."

She shrugs into the hip-length leather jacket, and I tell myself that it doesn't accentuate the sensual dip of her waist, the roundness of those perfect hips, or the lush perfection of her ass.

Goddamn, she really needs to go.

Pivoting, I head toward the foyer and front door. The scene of our two-year-old crime.

"Oh, I meant to tell you, I followed up on the other student who was teasing Rose." I skid to a halt, whipping around at the same time. India collides with me, unprepared for my abrupt about-face. Her palms slap to my chest, and I lock down the tortured groan climbing my throat like a cat scaling a scratching post. "Oh damn. Sorry." She drops her hands, rubbing her palms along her denim-covered thighs before she frowns and halts the gesture. "Anyway, I called her parents in and we had a long talk about bullying. I gave her detention for two days and she has to write Rose an apology letter."

Warmth surges through me, gratitude lodging in my throat. "Thank you." My lips twist into a deprecating, half-smile. "It seems like I'm saying that to you often lately."

She tilts her head to the side, her penny-colored eyes thoughtful as she studies me. I can't even count the number of times I've fantasized about her staring at my cock exactly like this as she tries to decide how she's going to swallow me down. Dream Me and Real Me don't give a fuck. Just as long as she lets me inside that mind-fuck of a mouth.

"Did you think I forgot?" she asks.

I hesitate. In each of our interactions, I've offended her. That's not my intention tonight, especially after we managed to get along the last few hours. But I can't lie to her either. "You have a lot of things on your plate," I hedge instead. "You're responsible for hundreds of kids, not just mine."

"We make time for what's important to us."

I slowly nod. "That's true. And I—" Breaking off, I drag a hand through my hair and expel a long, hard breath. "I know I apologized earlier, but I want to reiterate it. I'm sorry for being a dick. I don't want you to only be Rose's assistant principal; I want you to be her friend. She really likes you, and yeah, I lost my sister, but she lost her mother. And I can't relate to that like you can. If I'm honest..." I shake my head, not proud of my feelings and knee-jerk reaction outside the school. Not proud of how I lashed out at India like a spoiled kid instead of a grown-ass man. "If I'm honest, I was a little jealous that she felt comfortable going to you, talking to you, when she couldn't do that with me."

"Like I told you, that's only because she didn't want to make you upset or sad," she insists softly, fiercely. Lifting her arm, she settles her palm on my chest, and I stop myself from cuffing her wrist and removing her hand from me so she doesn't feel the rapid thudding of my heart. So she doesn't notice the effect her nearness has on my body. "She loves you, and in her own way was trying to protect you."

"I get that. Now," I add, and after another hesitation, I give in and cover her hand with mine.

Unbidden, I drop my gaze to my chest. Savor the sight of my fingers and palm fully enveloping hers. This is how we'd be in bed. I'd completely shelter her petite frame, leaving no part of her untouched, uncovered, unprotected. Scalding lust races through my veins, licking at that control I pride myself on. My gut clenches, and I fight the need simultaneously filling me and leaving me a throbbing, aching mess. Heat pounds in my cock, echoing my heartbeat—fast, hard, and unceasing.

Let her go. That's what I should do. What I fucking need to do. But my fingers won't cooperate, instead squeezing, imprisoning her palm against my chest.

Her eyes, so rich, so beautiful, darken. With surprise, yes, but also with the same emotion roaring through me like a wild, untamed beast. Lust. Hunger. Need.

"Don't look at me like that," I order, the command a step above guttural. "Close your eyes. Do it."

After a long second, she obeys, and a shudder ripples through me as a serrated growl rumbles up my chest and throat, punctuating the air between us.

"Why?" she breathes, and while her obedience thrills me, her refusal to completely surrender excites me. "Why do I have to close my eyes?"

I lean forward so our hands are wedged between us and with my free one I brush her thick curls back and away from her ear with more gentleness than I should be capable of in this moment.

"Because," I whisper, bringing our hips together so my erection is a hot, insistent presence against her belly and my thighs brace hers. Her gasp caresses my cheek, and a primal possessive urge spikes inside me. It's my cock cradled against the soft give of her stomach. My cock branding her. "Because you're looking at me like my dick is already filling up that undoubtedly tight-as-a-fucking-fist pussy," I grind out the accusation in her ear, my lips grazing the rim, and even that small, almost inconsequential touch is enough to have pre-cum dotting the head of my cock. "Your eyes are begging me to push into you until you can't take anymore. And then you go ahead and take more. They're begging me to break you, mold you. And depraved fuck that I am, I want to give it to you."

A sound that lies somewhere between a whine and a groan echoes in my ear. And I snap.

Two years of not seeing her should've cooled this clawing, raw, damn near savage need for her. With the exception of the dreams I had no influence over, I'd convinced myself it had eased. But it'd only lain dormant, waiting for her to return to wake it from its slumber, jack it back up to the howling, consuming lust that's making a laughing mockery of my control.

I drag my mouth down to her jaw, tracing the delicate line like it's a treasure map that will lead me to what I covet most—her mouth. With a hunger so strong it should terrify me, I take her lips. Cover them. Bruise them. Thrust my tongue between them.

A faint voice inside my head whispers to slow down, to gentle. But I can't. The sweet taste of her is riding my tongue now and there's no holding back. Because she's tilting her head and opening wider so I can claim more of her. Because she's sucking on me like I'm her favorite icy treat on a hot summer day. Because she's digging her fingernails into my back through my thermal shirt. No. No way in hell can I hold back when she's marking me as hard and thoroughly as I am her.

With one hand twisted in her hair, I release the other from in between our chests and drop it to the wide flare of her hip. God, her curves. They're so lush, so beautiful, so flagrantly feminine. I can't stop my fingers from travelling over the rounded flesh. From squeezing it, then following the sensual dip of her waist. From brushing over the gentle swell of her belly. From cupping the modest-but-perfect handful of her breast.

"*Fuck*," I snarl against her lips, just as she whimpers my name.

I've dreamed about touching her, imagined how her she would fit in my palm. But no fantasy could've prepared me for the reality of it. She's so soft, yet firm. And as I squeeze her, mold her, shape her, I silently admit to myself that I'm damned. Because the knowledge of how sensitive she is, how she arches into my caress, how her hard, little nipple impatiently thrusts against my palm is going to haunt me, a ghost that refuses to be exorcised.

I jerk my mouth from hers and tug up her shirt. Black-lace-covered bronze skin greets me, and my mouth waters as the tip of my cock weeps. I want to claim these beautiful tits with every part of my body—my mouth, my hands, my dick. Even as I yank down a cup, baring her to my greedy eyes, I envision straddling her chest and gliding my aching, thick cock up the valley between her breasts. Fucking her tits has just became a must-do on my bucket list—right after eating her pussy and burying myself balls-deep in it.

I stare at her brown, gleaming skin. Take in the swell of her flesh and the dark-brown beaded tip. Watch as it puckers even more, as if inviting me—no, pleading with me—to swallow her whole. And I can't deny anything when it comes to India.

"Asa," she whimpers, dragging her hands from my back to clutch my shoulders. "Please."

"What, baby girl?" I ask, goading her, knowing what she needs from me. But I want to hear those pretty, dirty words fall on my ears. I tear my gaze from her chest to her face so I can watch them form on her lips. "Please, what?"

A frown creases her forehead and her fingers flex against me. She trembles as if uttering the words aloud is too much.

"Ask for what you need from me, India," I demand, and as incentive, I brush my thumb across her nipple, drawing a ragged, agonized moan from her. *Goddamn.* That sound is so fucking pretty. I circle the tip, tracing the dark areola, wanting it to be my tongue. "Now," I rasp, desperate for that taste.

Her lashes flutter then lower, but her voice doesn't waver when she whispers, "Suck my breast, Asa. Please," she tacks on to the end. Her lashes lift, and I'm damn near drowning in the copper depths glazed with passion. With need. "Please make the hurt go away."

Fuck. Oh fuck.

Whether she's aware of it or not, she's hit my easy button. I would move a goddamn mountain to relieve her pain. To ease it. And I would level that same mountain to the ground if she would let me be the cause of the sensual agony darkening her eyes.

I want to be her tormentor and her savior.

Lowering my head, I bury my face between her breasts, breathing in her sultry, musky scent. Jasmine and rain. Perspiration and skin. With a growl, I turn my head, capture her nipple between my lips. Draw hard on it. Tongue it. Scrape my teeth over it.

Her hands abandon my shoulders for my head, her fingers twisting in the strands, tugging. Each pinprick across my scalp enflames my hunger, and I dine on her. My fingers fumble for the other breast. Hook under the bra cup. Yank—

"Uncle Asa!"

Rose's shout from down the hall douses me in a sheet of ice.

Shit.

Wrenching away from India, I stare down at her, wondering if my eyes are as wide, as filled with shock and lust. Pain ricochets from me, the abrupt jolt of emerging from such pleasure to cold loneliness a blow to my system. For a moment, my mind scrambles to compute that I'm no longer touching her. That her scent isn't in my nose, my mouth.

"Uncle Asa!" Rose's voice is closer, and panic spirals up from my clenching gut to my chest, exploding like shrapnel.

Exhaling a rough, jagged breath, I drag a hand through my hair and stalk around India toward the hall, cutting Rose off mid-way. And hopefully granting India enough time to right the mess I made of her.

"What is it, Sweet Pea?"

She shoots me a disgruntled look, crossing her arms over her pink robe. "I was calling you *forever*. Where were you?"

"Saying goodbye to India." I'm going to hell for lying to my niece. Especially when I can still taste India with the mouth that's doing the fibbing. "What's up?"

"I forgot to get my towel from the closet."

"I'll get it for you. Go get in the shower and I'll leave it on the back of the toilet for you."

She nods slowly. "Okay. I want the one with Belle on it," she instructs me, eyeing me as if she can't trust me to choose the correct Disney princess.

"Got it. I'll be right there."

Yes, I'm rushing my niece along so I can return to India and try to rectify the damage I've wreaked on an already tenuous truce. And as I pivot and head back toward her, the "I'm sorry" is already crawling up my throat and crowding into my mouth. I'm familiar with its bitter flavor. Just as I'm well-acquainted with the guilt churning in my gut.

Jesus. I scrub a hand down my face. I lost complete control. Again. One taste of her and I didn't care about who she was—whom she belongs to. Because it doesn't matter if she and Jessie are no longer together, she will always belong to him. She can never be mine because she was his first. He's my brother in every way but blood, and to be with India means betraying him.

And that I can't do.

He's never failed to have my back. After my football career littered the ground in ashes, he helped me buy the garage when no bank would touch me or my credit. Since then, I've repaid the loan back with the interest he didn't want, but still... If it wasn't for him, I would be working for someone else, earning the bare minimum instead of being my own boss.

He's family. And after Mona, I can't lose one more person I love.

But my throbbing body, my pounding cock competes with regret. India is... she's my weakness. My lust for her my personal Sword of Damocles, hanging over my head, ready to fall and pierce me at any given time.

And fuck if I don't want to be run through with it.

Sighing, I rub my hand over the back of my neck. "India, I—"

The words stutter, than disappear from my lips. Because she's gone. Just her jasmine and fresh rain scent lingers in the small entryway that's once more the site of our fall from grace.

"Goddamn it," I growl, battling the urge to yank the door open and see if her car is still backing out of my driveway. So I can—what? Catch up with her? Make this worse by apologizing? By calling her a mistake again?

I have no idea, no fucking clue what I'm doing.

But one thing's for certain. If I touch her one more time in this foyer, I'm going to have to tear the fucker down with my bare hands.

5

Asa

"Damn, Ace. I can't tell you how much I've missed this." Jessie grins, clapping me on my shoulder and squeezing. "'Preciate you coming out with me tonight."

I shake my head, signaling to Tracy, one of the regular bartenders at The Hammerhead, our local—hell, *only*—bar. I circle a finger over our beers, ordering another round. Tracy tips her chin up, acknowledging me before finishing pulling a draft for another customer.

I snort, lifting my beer bottle and draining the last of the alcohol. "Yeah, well, you know I'll always make time for you in my jam-packed schedule. Right between a paint job and an alignment."

Jessie laughs, his green eyes crinkling at the corners. I'm not into men, but looking at my best friend, I get why women lose their damn minds over him. He's maintained his quarterback physique—wide-shouldered, slim-hipped, with not an ounce of fat on him—and with his close-cropped, dark-blond hair and pretty-boy face, he's as popular and in demand now as he was while playing for the Rams during his five-year career. Now, instead of throwing balls on Sunday mornings or Monday nights, he could be found on ESPN as a sportscaster. He'd coasted the transition from player to journalist with an ease that defined Jessie. Determination. Focus. And a charm that could make him a douche if it wasn't so genuine.

Sometimes, I catch myself envying him. Part of me can't help but imagine sitting beside him at that roundtable, commentating and discussing the sport we both love. Or better yet, playing on the field together, wide receiver to his quarterback. After all, the dream had been to play side-by-side in the league. But only one of us had made that fantasy a reality. I'm happy for him, for his career and success both on and off the field. But yeah... I can't help but think of the what-ifs...

Tracy sets down our cold, fresh bottles in front of us with a wink. Though she's only a few years older than our twenty-nine, she's been a staple in the bar as long as we've been coming here. She and her twin sister took over the place from their father about three years back, and with live music on the weekend, a separate section for pool, and Hump Day half-price drinks, they've really turned around a bar that had been one more police visit and condom machine away from being a dive.

"Here you go, guys." Stacking her crossed arms on the bar top, she leans forward, pinning me with a teasing, narrowed glare. "Asa, why is it that I only see you in here when this one," she jerks her chin in Jessie's direction, "deigns to come down from Bristol to visit us peons? I'm starting to get offended." The smile flirting with the corner of her mouth belies her words, but I can't deny the truth of her accusation.

Between Rose, the regular responsibilities of the shop, and steadily building our clientele for the restoration side of the garage, I don't have much free time.

"*Deigns* to come down?" Jessie repeats, chuckling. "Now you're making me sound like a douche."

She shrugs a slim shoulder. "If the canoe fits..."

I snicker, trading the empty out for the new beer and taking a long sip. "No worries, man," I say, slapping him on the back of the shoulder with my free hand. "Us peons are the forgiving sort. It's our peasant stock."

"Fuck you." He grins, shaking his head.

Laughing, Tracy slaps the bar top. "Just holler if you need anything else," she tosses at us, before striding away to help another customer.

"Is it me, or does she just get sexier every time we come in here?" he muses, staring after the slender woman.

With her sleek, dark hair cut into an asymmetrical bob that brushes her shoulders, gleaming, mahogany skin bared by a black tank top with the bar's logo stretched across her generous breasts, and tight jeans that hug her rounded hips, yeah, she's hot as hell.

But she does nothing for me. Because apparently my cock prefers petite women with tight, gravity-defying curls, curves that would make a racetrack groan in jealousy, and eyes the color of freshly minted pennies.

No, not women. Woman. One.

India.

Fuck. My fingers tighten around my beer, and I lift it for another deep swallow. But the cold, yeasty alcohol hitting my gut can't extinguish the heat simmering in my veins. Still, thinking about my best friend's ex while sitting right damn next to him is bad form. Hell, it's lunacy.

Especially since Jessie isn't over India.

Yes, it's been two years and by no means has he been a monk, but Jessie hasn't been in a serious relationship since India walked away from him. And then there'd been the time I'd flown out to Connecticut to visit him for a weekend. After drinking a little too much, he'd confessed his love for her and how he fucked up the best thing in his life, and he wished he could go back and undo the past. It'd been so goddamn hard sitting there, listening to him pouring his heart out about her, all the while knowing I'd kissed her. I'd touched her. I knew with startling and vivid clarity that she tasted like the freshest water and the dirtiest sex.

I have no business possessing that knowledge. And the fact that I did made me the shittiest friend. The shittiest person.

"So, what's up with you?" Jessie twists on the stool, propping an arm on the bar. He studies me, wearing a small half smile. "I talked with your mom. Right after I thanked her for keeping Rose for the night so we could have this," he waved his arm out, encompassing the bar, "she told me about my little niece getting in trouble in school. Apparently, she slapped the shit out of a little girl?"

Panic explodes in my chest like an atom bomb, mushrooming to fill my rib cage, my throat, my gut. Had Mom mentioned India? Did Jessie suspect that I was lying to him, even if by omission?

"Jess..." I murmur.

"She also told me what the girl said to her. Now, other than the field, you know I don't advocate violence, but..." He smirks. "Between me, you, and this beer, that girl had it coming."

Relief crashes over me, and if I wasn't sitting, my ass would be hitting the floor. He doesn't know. For some reason, Mom neglected to tell him about India's position at the school. Maybe because she thought I had, or she just didn't want to bring up the hurtful past with Jessie—whatever. I'm just so damn thankful.

Snapping right at the heels of that gratitude, though, is shame. I'm a coward. Since I walked into the school's office for that meeting and came face-to-face with India, I've talked with Jessie a handful of times. And each time, I convinced myself I would tell him about India being back in town. And each time I dug up an excuse to put it off. He's about to go on air. I can't distract him now. Or, he sounds so happy, just like his old self. I can't bring her up and take that away from him. Or, he's in Connecticut. There isn't shit he can do about it, so why hurt him with this news?

Yeah, I'm so damn thoughtful. I'm also the king of excuses. And when it comes down to it? A chicken shit.

Pike's End is a small-as-hell town. If I don't tell him now, someone else inadvertently will. I can't let him be blindsided like that. That was my intention when I suggested coming to The Hammerhead for beers. And now that we're here, I'm out of reasons to keep him in the dark. He needs to know.

"Yeah, Rose got a week of in-school detention because of her latest stunt. But the vice principal was understanding about her situation." I swallow. Hard. Setting my bottle on the bar top, I bow my head and drag in a deep breath. Now or never. And never isn't an option. "Speaking of the vice principal... Jessie, there's something I—"

"*The fuck.*"

His harsh whisper has my head jerking up. But he's not looking at me. His wide gaze is fixed across the room toward the entrance of the bar. My heart thuds in dull, heavy beats, filling my head, echoing in my ears. The bottom of my stomach plummets, and I slowly follow the direction he's staring, because in my soul, I know who will be standing there.

I know who's placed that stricken, gutted expression on my friend's face.

"*India?*" he rasps.

My eyes briefly close. It isn't just her name that shivers through me like ghostly, skeletal fingers trailing down my spine. It's *her* name in *his* voice. That serrated, hollow voice that contains an awful note of wonder... of hope.

As if she heard her name over the Friday night noise of the bar, she glances in our direction. And freezes.

Apologies to her, to Jessie—to God, to fucking everybody—tumble over themselves in my head. I had no idea she would be here tonight, but somehow, I'm flaying myself alive for unintentionally arranging this impromptu reunion.

Tearing my gaze from her, I take in the people gathered around her. The office assistant from the school—I'd recognize the combination of dreads and funky glasses anywhere. Lena. That's her name. The men on either side of them, though...

A dark, ugly emotion stirs behind my sternum. An emotion I have no right to feel. But that fact doesn't stop the stain of it from spreading like an oil slick across my chest, up into my throat. Jealously. Anger. An almost feral possessiveness that has me seconds from stalking over there, wrapping my hand around the back of her neck and slamming my mouth down on hers. Grinding my cock against her belly. Fucking rub my scent on her like a goddamn animal.

Jesus.

What the hell is wrong with me? She's. Not. Mine. She can never be mine.

And all I need to do is glance at the man next to me, take in his stunned, shattered face, and be reminded why.

"What the fuck? India?" Jessie repeats, rising from his stool.

I clap my hand on his shoulder, exerting enough pressure to still him. His head whips toward me, his eyes narrowed. As if he's restraining the need to tear away from me and charge across the room to his ex-girlfriend.

"Jessie, wait," I say, keeping my voice low, hopefully calm.

"Are you ser—?" His eyes flare wide, then narrow again. "You knew," he growls. "You knew she was here, and you didn't say one goddamn word. How long?" he demands. "How long have you been lying to me?"

Heaving a sigh, I risk releasing him, and thrust my fingers through my hair, gripping the strands tight until tiny spikes of pain punish my scalp.

"I meant to tell you, Jess," I say. "I've been trying to for a week now."

"Trying?" he snaps, lowering back to the stool and leaning into my space. His dark brows arrow down over eyes glittering with anger. "What the fuck does that mean? What's so hard about saying, *Hey, Jess. India's back. Thought you should know.*"

"Because it's her. Because it's India. That's why it was hard."

He stares at me for several long seconds. Even

though the bar rings with chatter, laughter, and the rock music over the PA system, the silence between us blares, deafening me. Slowly, the fury ebbs then drains from his gaze and expression. A profound sorrow, so deep it's hard to look at, etches his face.

"Yeah," he murmurs. "Yeah, I get it." Turning from me, he snatches up his beer and downs about half of it before smacking it back down. "Talk," he orders, still not meeting my gaze.

"She's Rose's vice principal. She came back here at the beginning of the school year, but I didn't find out until I went up to the school for the meeting last Friday," I explain.

"Has she talked to you at all?" he grates out, eyes still trained on the scarred bar top. His fingers clasp the half-full bottle as if it's a lifeline.

I hesitate, and that slick, grimy coat thickens. Because I'm going to lie. Even if it's by omission, I'm going to lie to my best friend. But there's no way in hell I can tell him about Wednesday night or the kiss afterward.

"She has a little. Like where she's been the past two years. She went to Seattle and finished up her degree there. When the assistant principal position came open here, she accepted."

"That's it?" He clears his throat. "She didn't ask..."

He trails off, but he doesn't need to finish his sentence, I already know how it ends.

"No," I say, voice low. "She didn't ask about you."

A muscle jumps along his tightly clenched jaw. "Right," he mutters. His fingers drum on the bar top. And I stare at him, body tense. Ready to... what? Grab him if he heads over there toward India? Follow him to protect her from him? Protect him from himself. *Dammit.* I just don't fucking know.

Unbidden, my attention shifts from him, and I scan the room, locating India and her group at a middle table. I have a perfect view of her profile—and of the asshole sitting on the other side of her with his arm slung around the back of her chair, his hand resting on her upper arm.

Who is he? How long has she been dating him? And how could she let me fuck her mouth just two days ago when she's been seeing this guy?

And I have no right to ask these questions. No right to the answers. And that I'm even wondering them with Jessie sitting right beside me drags me down to a whole lower level of bastard.

Disgusted with myself, I start to turn back to my beer, but at that moment, India glances at me. And God help me, but I can't look away. Not when her mouth firms into a hard line. Not when she pushes back from the table and rises.

Not when she winds her way through tables and customers and approaches us.

And not when she stands beside me, her scent a gentle tease under the smells of yeasty beer, grilling burgers, and fried bar food and fresh oak from the "game" room the twins had constructed a couple of weeks ago. Yeah, how pathetic does it make me that I can still identify her skin-warmed, addictive fragrance?

Pretty fucking pathetic.

"Asa," she greets me in a tight voice that practically vibrates with tension. At the sound, Jessie's head jerks up, and he whips around on the stool, facing her. His chest rises and falls on fast, silent breaths as he stares at her. "Jessie," she says in that same taut tone.

"Hello, India," he murmurs, and that same visceral

reaction that surged within me at the sight of her with another man roars back to life.

She was *his*.

He knows how it feels to be on the receiving end of her smiles, her laughter, her easy affection—her love. He knows the beauty and security of being enfolded in her arms. He knows the peace of falling asleep, wrapped around her after the pleasure of being buried deep inside her body.

He knows what I never will—what I never can. And yet, I still want to drag her behind me, hiding her so he can't look at her with that tender warmth and possessiveness gleaming in his eyes.

I can't do this. I can't—

"I'll be back," I grind out, shooting to my feet. Snatching my beer up, I don't look back to gauge their reaction to my abrupt departure. I can't bear the longing and heat in my friend's gaze.

And I don't trust what I might do if I spy the same emotion in India's copper eyes.

~

India

He left me.

Asa left me alone with the last person I wanted to come face-to-face with. Reason argues that the hurt throbbing in my chest like a toothache is unreasonable. Any witnesses for this long-time-in-coming confrontation would be awkward as hell for all parties. And it's not like Jessie is a stranger—well, he didn't used to be.

But my heart is telling that reason to go screw itself. I need Asa's quiet, stalwart strength behind me as

I stare into my past. As I meet the green gaze and beautiful face of the man I believed would be my future, my forever. I need Asa's presence that both stirs and calms me.

I need *him*.

And fuck him for leaving me. Proving once again where I fall on his list of priorities.

If there's one thing my mother's death, working two jobs to pay for college, and surviving Jessie's betrayal has taught me, it's that I can't count on anyone but myself. And I'm more than enough.

Squaring my shoulders, I hike my chin up, not flinching from Jessie's unwavering inspection of me. He's so... familiar. A pang echoes in my chest. Once, he was my shelter, my safe place. Until he became the storm that ripped away the moorings of my life.

I mourned that more than anything. After Mom died, I lost my security, my rock. And then he came along, and I lowered my guard to trust again, to believe again. And losing him—that haven—thrust me back to when I was sixteen, grieving, disillusioned, and alone.

Now, I'm no longer in that dark place. And I will never allow anyone to drag me there again. Giving someone that kind of control over my heart, my *world*?

No. Only I can be trusted with that kind of power.

"India." He shakes his head. "Jesus, I can't believe you're here in front of me. That it's really you." His emerald gaze roams my face, lingering on my mouth. I wait for the flare of heat, the old desire that used to fill me whenever I was within four feet of him.

But... nothing. Well, it's not *his* lips I'm recalling. Not the memory of *his* kiss that flickers across my mind, that has desire licking at my belly and between my legs. It's his best friend's.

Guilt slicks across my chest, and I turn away from Jessie to signal the bartender and order a glass of red wine. Maybe I can get a two-fer, and the alcohol will help wash away the guilt and the memories of Asa's taste—and the remorse that had darkened his eyes.

Because you're looking at me like my dick is already filling up that undoubtedly tight as a fucking fist pussy... Your eyes are begging me to push into you until you can't take anymore. They're begging me to break you, mold you. And depraved fuck that I am, I want to give it to you.

His filthy, insanely hot words from that night whisper through my head as if he's standing behind me, uttering them in that gravel-roughened voice, and my sex clenches as if pleading for him to do just what he described. My thighs tremble, and I'm getting wet from the memory alone.

God, how many times have I imagined him pushing, breaking, molding, while I tired my clit out with my hands, my vibrator? Cruel of him to plant that image in my brain and then reject me.

Again.

Hurt and anger mingle with the lust. When am I going to learn when it comes to him? Pathetically, I have no answer. Especially with his best friend, my ex, sitting next to me, his gaze on me. Shit. Only when my glass is set in front of me and the cool, dry wine is sliding down my throat do I return to face Jessie.

"You look well, Jessie," I say, shoving the words past my constricted throat. "I was sorry to hear about your injury and early retirement. I know how much the game meant to you."

All true. I didn't blame football or his love of it for the ending of our relationship. He got caught up in the trappings that came with it. And hadn't been strong enough to keep his dick in his pants and some random chick's mouth off it.

"Yeah, it was hard, but with the sportscasting, I can still enjoy it. Just in a different way. Truthfully, India," he huffed out a low, rough laugh, tunneling his fingers through his dark-blond hair, "after you left, my heart wasn't in it like it used to be. Knowing I'd allowed it to fuck up what we had—"

"No, Jess," I interrupted, holding up a hand to stop the excuse hovering on his lips. "The game didn't fuck us up. You did. Own it."

"India..."

"No," I say again, shaking my head. I told myself I was coming over here just to speak, so the cold front that stretched from the table to the bar didn't leave me with frost bite. To show him and myself that I'm over him, that he no longer possesses any power of me or my feelings. Not to crawl through my past with this man, to resurrect old shit. But the words churn inside me, gaining speed and strength, and they break free like swollen rapids contained behind a steadily splintering dam. Words I didn't get to say because I'd left this town and him in the dead of night. "The game wasn't engaged to me. The game didn't promise to love me, to stay faithful to me. The game wasn't my best friend, my lover, my everything. *You* were."

Pain slashes across his handsome face, and an instinctive apology dances on my tongue. Deliberately hurting him is not my aim, and the part of myself that still recognizes him as the man who once held my heart yearns to comfort him. But I lock that half down.

"I didn't come over here to rehash our history. Or to throw blame in your face, Jessie. And honestly, I don't hate you anymore. I let go of that a while ago.

For myself. Because I couldn't start a new life still holding on to the old one."

"You mean still holding on to me," he adds, a strain of bitterness threading through his voice.

"Yes." There's no point in denying it.

"And what if I wanted you to hold onto me? To us?" he demanded, leaning toward me, that same intensity that used to radiate from him when he played football pinned on me. Who am I kidding? That intensity had been for me, too. As much as I preferred to forget it, when we were together, I used to be on the receiving end of all his focus. And I'd loved it. A faint echo of how much I'd loved it rippled through me now. But not strong enough to make me fall back into the lovely black hole that had been Jessie Reynolds. "You never gave me a chance to make it right. To fix us. One mistake. One, out of the four years we were together. I deserved the chance, baby."

"You deserved what I needed to fight my way through to the other side of being good again. To survive the pain the heartbreak. And what I needed was time and space. Without you. It ceased being about you, what you wanted when your side-chick messaged me. Dammit," I bite out. Closing my eyes, I sink my teeth into my bottom lip and turn away. "Jess, I don't want to do this, okay? Not now and not here."

Not ever.

I slide off the bar stool, but his hand shoots out, gently wrapping around my wrist. I glance down, again waiting for that... something. The desire that used to stir in me for him. The love that used to bind me to him. But again... nothing. I imagined this day and had always wondered if that adoration would swell in my chest, would make me a slave to my emotions.

But no. I'm free.

And I'm both relieved and strangely, sad.

"India, please," he whispers. "You said you don't hate me. Maybe we can start there." His green gaze searches my face, touches on my eyes, lips, chin then back to my eyes. "I'm so incredibly sorry I hurt you, baby. I've never forgiven myself for it. And I've never stopping thinking about you, wondering where you were, if you were all right. India, maybe I don't deserve it, but I'm still asking. Us being here tonight..." He shakes his head. "I refuse to believe it was a mistake. Please, give me a chance to do what I couldn't two years ago. Make things right between us. What we had —you can't convince me you don't feel anything for me. Not after who we were to each other."

There'd been moments after I left Pike's End that I would've caved and gone back to him if he'd appeared on my friend's apartment doorstep and uttered these same words to me. Just to stop the pain. But I'm not that woman anymore. I've crawled through to the other side, and the truth is, I'm scared. Scared to trust, to be vulnerable and dependent on another person again.

Especially one who's already betrayed me.

"Who we *were*, Jessie," I murmur, gently twisting my arm to extricate my wrist from his grip. "There is no going back. I've moved on. You should, too."

I turn and walk back to the table with Lena, her cousin and brother. What started as a fun night has soured, and it sits on my stomach like curdled milk.

"You okay?" Lena asks, as soon as I sink down onto the chair, her hazel eyes concerned behind her blue-rimmed glasses.

"Yeah, I'm..."

Movement snags my attention out the corner of

my eye. Asa pushes off the far wall, and even though he's half-enshrouded in shadows, I *feel* his gaze on me like a heavy palm. Over my face, my throat, my suddenly tingling breasts, and lower, to my achingly empty pussy. That quick, he lights a fire in me that only he can extinguish, but he refuses to do it.

And after talking with Jessie for the first time in two years, I understand why.

I do. But it still doesn't change the stark truth that crouches between us, rattling like an agitated snake.

The man I want won't allow himself to have me because I'm Jessie's girl. In his eyes, I always will be.

"I'm fine."

6

India

When the doorbell echoes inside my cozy, rented bungalow several hours later, I'm not surprised. Still, my feet don't move forward. Instead, I stare at the door, picturing the man on the other side. The broad shoulders, the wide chest that probably spans the width of the frame. The big hands that once palmed footballs and held me just as easily. The thick trunks of his thighs that had strained against denim as he'd pushed himself from the bar stool. The frown that, at times, seemed to be surgically implanted on his face.

God, that frown.

It did things to me.

Made me fantasize about if he'd wear it while sliding inside of me for the first time. If it'd etch his forehead while he came...

Frown porn.

Oh yeah, I'm a bit sick. And apparently, horny as fuck.

A hard, loud knock reverberates through my small foyer. Asa not only has the build and scowl of a bull, but the stubbornness of one, too. He's not going away. If I had the sense God gave a gnat, I'd keep the door shut and pretend I don't hear the impatient summons.

But God and I both know when it comes to this man, I'm not smart. I haven't been in two years... and counting.

Cursing myself for being about eleven-ty different kinds of fools, I unlock the door and pull it open. Asa lifts his head, and eyes brewing with grey clouds stare back at me. His hands clutch either side of the jam, and I don't know if he's holding himself up... or forcing himself not to throw his body away from my door. Away from me.

"India."

His dark rasp licks over my skin, and shivers dance my spine, tingling at the base. I hate that he drags this response from me. Hate that those all-too-perceptive eyes note every tremble.

"It's late, Asa. What do you want?" I cross my arms over my chest just in case he thinks it's his presence, the looming of his big body that damn near shuts out the sky behind him, that has my nipples poking against my bra and shirt and not the cool October air.

"Let me in, India," he murmurs, and the soft voice coupled with the silver-thin thread of steel has me standing on the knife's edge of telling him to fuck right off or stepping back and giving him anything he wants. Begging him to take anything he wants.

Jesus. I don't need a pied piper to lead me to my doom. I'm doing a bang-up job all by myself.

I recognize the danger of letting him into my space. Of allowing his presence to imprint itself on the place where I come home every night. The place I come to dream. And yet, my feet are shuffling backward, my hand is holding the door open, and my pride is embarking on a suicide mission.

"What do you want, Asa?" I demand. Yes, I just invited him in, but I want him gone. The longer he's here, the higher my chances of committing some monumentally stupid and unforgivable act.

He closes the door behind him with a soft *snick* and doesn't immediately answer. Instead, he silently studies me, and I fight not to fidget. To pretend as if I don't feel that unwavering, penetrating gaze stroke over the shelf of my cheekbones, the slope of my nose, the line of my jaw, the curve of my mouth, like physical caresses.

"Are you okay?" he asks.

Such three innocuous words. Strung together, they're an expression of concern. They're also the match to the powder keg of my temper.

I. Snap.

"Am I okay?" I whisper, slowly lowering my arms down to my side. "You mean, am I okay because I bumped into my ex, whom I haven't seen in two years? Or because that same man who broke my heart wants me to give him another chance?" Asa's face tightens and his full lips flatten into a hard line. The gleam in his narrowed gaze should give me pause, but fuck that. I'm on a roll. "Or are you asking because you, who knew all of this, abandoned me? Leaving me alone with him."

"And what did you tell him?" he murmurs, the grit in that softly spoken question rubbing over my skin, leaving pebbled flesh behind.

"Wh-what?" I stutter.

"What did you tell Jessie when he asked for another chance with you?" he clarified in that same tone that could've ground gravel into smooth-as-glass sand.

"What are you hoping for, Asa?" I cock my head, studying his face for some clue inside that head of his. Past the shadows that cloud the truth like storm clouds hide the sun. "What answer do you want to hear? That I told him no? Or that I said yes, so you can be a martyr for your best friend." I loose a chuckle that scrapes my throat, suddenly tired. And empty. "Go home, Asa."

He doesn't move, and his silent refusal to leave strikes a match to my anger again.

"I said, *go*."

"No." The answer is flat, blunt. And a whole lot of "no way in hell."

"Is this fun for you?" I hiss. "Pull me close, push me away. Is this some fucked up form of exercise?"

He moves so fast, all I have time to do is gasp. Damn. For such a big man, he's quick. His hand snakes out, wrapping around the nape of my neck and dragging me forward, so close our foreheads bump and our breath mingles, mates.

"Don't stop now. Give it to me," I sneer, the effect slightly ruined by my soft, rapid pants of breath.

I'm shamelessly goading him to... what? Give me the truth? His kiss? His cock? With lust sizzling through my veins and eating me up in great, gulping bites, I can't honestly pinpoint what I want. What I'm inciting him to do.

"Shut up," he softy orders, but there's no mistaking or missing the filaments of steel that knit through it.

"I don't have to—"

"Shut. The fuck. Up." His grip on my nape tightens. Not hard enough to hurt—Asa would never cause me pain, at least not physically—but enough to startle me into doing what he ordered. Shut the fuck up. "Do you want to know why I got up and left? Why I walked away? Because it was either that or stay there and punch the man I consider closer than a brother in the goddamn face if he continued to stare at you like he was remembering every time he was inside you. Like he was hearing the little whimper you make when you're hot and wet. Like he wanted to hear it again while being balls-deep inside you... again."

He rolls his forehead against mine, his eyes squeezing shut for a moment before opening and burning into mine. Even in spite of the shock seizing me in its icy hold, a thick, humid heat swamps me. I'm fire and ice. Numb and a mass of overly exposed nerves.

"I couldn't sit there another moment and stare into that face, knowing he's imagining what I can only dream about. What torments me every goddamn night. What has me waking up, fucking the hell out of my fist. He's had this pussy." He doesn't roll his hips forward. Hell no. He punches them against me so I'm branded by his dick, even through our clothes. That big, thick length propels the breath from my body as if he's thrust deep inside me and bumped my damn lungs. "He's had this mouth." His lifts his free hand, presses the pad of his thumb to the middle of my bottom lip and tugs. Then pushes his thumb inside my mouth, gliding it over my tongue where it sits, heavy and tantalizing like a threat... and a promise. "He knows the feel of this." He slowly thrusts the digit back and forth over between my lips, and I can't help but suck, taste the sandalwood-and-earth scent that clings to him from his skin. His growl relays his approval. His need. The flick of my tongue conveys mine. "He's had it all. Wants it again, and part of me almost fucking hates him for it."

Lust mingles with hurt, bitterness, and yes, God

help me, triumph, to hear him admit that he resents his friend because of me. I'm not proud of it. Dammit, *I'm not*. It makes me petty and a fool. Because in the end, I harbor no doubts who would win in the tug of war between me and Jessie. Hell, there's no competition, because it's a stacked fight. Jessie would win every time. There's a bond there between them that's unbreakable, and Asa wouldn't allow me to come between them. He'd never choose me.

Yet, knowing he wanted to go to battle over me...

This is what this man did to me. Had me turning in my *Fight the patriarchy!* T-shirt for a white, flowing *peplos*, while some man with a Medusa head fought a Titan on my behalf. Damn damsel in distress.

Self-disgust streaks through me, temporarily capsizing the hunger still lapping at me, and I wrench my head back. His hold on my nape tightens, controlling the movement, but at least he isn't penetrating my mouth any longer. Though, the phantom weight of him still lingers on my tongue. And the flavor of him remains behind, a delicious aftertaste I wish I could banish.

Lie.

Wedging my hands between our bodies, I curl my fingers against the rock-hard wall of his chest. He's elemental—earth and flame. Stone and fire. He burns my palms, my fingers, even as he provides a firm, unyielding foundation for them. What would it be like to curl up against him, to lie across him and have those big, heavy arms close around me?

Nothing could touch me in his bed.

Nothing would dare.

I would be utterly safe under him. Over him.

And that safety is just as addictive as the thought

of him driving deep and branding me with that wide, big cock.

"Why are you really here?" I rasp, panic thickening my voice. Panic and desperation. And their origin story is the same. Drive him away before he can hurt me. Change me. Persuade me to capitulate the very small remaining distance into this insane need that threatens to swamp me with every breath, every heartbeat.

"India," Asa breathes, his grey gaze roaming my face.

His signature frown starts to lower his brows again, but I shake my head. Yes, probably too hard.

"No, I heard you. But tell me why you're *really* here. Be honest about why you came into my house hot. You want to use anger as a reason to kiss me? To fuck me? So afterward, you can blame it on the anger and absolve yourself from guilt by convincing yourself you slipped again? You weren't in control? Well, sorry. Go get your fix and absolution somewhere else."

My chest rises and falls on jagged pants, mimicking the breaths that careen out of him. He stares at me, his storm-heavy scrutiny a weight on my face—one I can't escape.

Slowly, he straightens, lifting his head and releasing his hand from the back of my neck. Then he shifts backward. One step. Then another. And one more.

I wanted space. And he gives it to me. But now, I sink my teeth into the tender skin of the inside of my bottom lip to keep myself from begging him to come back. To touch me again. To let me inhale his rich, dark scent again. To taste him again.

"I shouldn't be here," he says, and the rumble in his voice is sensory foreplay. I wrap my arms around myself in a flimsy offering of protection against it. "If I were any kind of friend, I wouldn't be," he adds, and there's no mistaking or missing the self-loathing there. "But that didn't—couldn't—keep me away from your doorstep. You want me to be honest, India? You, who run away each time any situation gets too hot, too difficult? Okay, baby girl. I'll be honest."

A knot of unease pulls taut in my stomach and I tighten my arms around me. Part of me wants to order him to shut up, to not speak. That I rescind my demand for honesty. Because honesty costs—and not just from the one telling it. There's a price exacted from the hearer, too. But I didn't think about that before I got reckless with my mouth.

Yet, the other half of me remains silent, waiting to hear his truth. Hungry to hear it. No matter the consequences.

"Yeah, I showed up here angry. For the reason I already told you. But also because of what I saw at that bar. You, with some random guy, his arm around you, not two days after my mouth had been on you and I can still feel your nipple on my tongue. Do I have a right to want to grab him up and tell him to keep his fucking hands to himself? No. But that didn't stop me from wanting it. Didn't stop me from having to talk myself down from asking you who he was and why was he touching you."

His frown has become fierce again, those eyes glittering like polished steel. He slightly leans forward, and though it's impossible, I swear I can feel the heat emanating from his big body.

"Do I want to fuck you? Yeah. I do. At this moment, I want it more than my relationship with my best friend. What does that say about me, India? What kind of man does that make me? What kind of friend?

So that guilt you mentioned? It's there. But I don't need any convincing to get my dick inside you. It's where I want to be. Where I think I'll go fucking insane if I don't. Because you are right about one thing. You are my fix. Just a goddamn kiss and I'm addicted. I need more. That's why I'm here, India. For more."

The air stutters and stalls in my lungs somewhere around *I don't need any convincing to get my dick inside you*. Liquid heat floods me, pouring through my veins, and transforming me into a living torch. I'm lit up, and that heat centers between my legs where my sex pulses, aches with a wonderfully terrible emptiness to be filled.

To be fucked.

"You want more?" I whisper.

"Yeah, baby girl. Fuck, yeah," he says, his voice the consistency of churned up gravel. "You going to give me more?"

"Yes." I am. It might damn us both to hell, but I am.

Tomorrow, I'll regret this. It's inevitable. Especially when the first time comes that he denies me in front of Jessie, or coldly relegates me to his friend's ex again. But right now, I don't care. I just want his hands on me.

"Then come give it to me."

I know what he's doing. What he needs from me.

To make the first move. To come take from him.

My feet move before my brain can send a cautionary message to stop, think, reconsider, but my body doesn't heed it. And within seconds, I stand before him, tilting my head back to meet that piercing, unblinking gaze. Maybe he can read the hunger on my face, glimpse it in my eyes, because he moves that last inch separating us until his chest presses against mine.

His powerful thighs bracket mine. His cock nudges my belly, a brand that sears my skin through his jeans and my shirt. Greed for him—for that hard, cruel, yet carnal mouth, those large hands, that seductive woodsy and earthen taste—ripples through and over me, and I shudder with it.

"Give me more," he orders, and I barely understand him, his voice is so rough. "And don't hold anything back."

His words unlock something in me—something I wasn't aware had been trapped, imprisoned. But he released it in that moment, and in the living room of my rental house, I feel freer than I ever have in my life. I can do what I want. Be whom I desire.

Well, I want to do Asa, and I desire to be the woman who isn't afraid to claim what—or whom—she longs for.

Not breaking our visual connection, I sink to my knees.

The snag of his breath breaks on the air, and that's his only movement as I tilt my head back and drink him in. The stark beauty, harshened even further by the lust stamped on his face. The blazing desire brightening his eyes to liquid steel. That same desire drawing his full mouth tight.

I lift my trembling hands to the leather belt at his waist, and with suddenly clumsy hands, loosen it. The task takes me twice as long as it should, but finally, I finish and reach for the button and zipper on his jeans.

"India."

Another shiver trips down my spine at that voice... or it could be the press of his huge, scarred hand over both of mine.

"India, you don't have to do this," he says in a low voice.

Surprise and, yes, a little bit of hurt, jolts through me. "I know that. I *want to*." My fingers involuntarily flex under his.

"Do you?"

His gaze narrows on me, and that look, this questioning, should douse the hunger clawing at me. But just the opposite. On my knees in front of him, that dominance pouring off of him demanding the truth even though he hasn't touched me yet... My pussy spasms, reminding me of how empty it is, just in case I'd forgotten. Which I haven't.

"Yes." I curl my fingers around his waistband and trap a whimper when my skin strokes over the unyielding skin of his lower abdomen. "Yes, I do."

"Then why are you shaking so hard you can barely undo a simple belt?" he demanded.

"Because I want it too much," I confess with complete honesty, refusing to hold anything back here. "You make me clumsy."

I didn't think it possible, but his face hardens even further, those eyes... Good God, those eyes.

He drops to his knees in front of me so swiftly, I reach for him, unable to contain my small, startled cry, as concern for his old football injury rushes through me. But Asa doesn't seem to care as he cups the back of my neck, dragging me forward the few inches separating us. Tunnelling the other hand in my hair, he jerks my head back and crushes his mouth to mine.

This.

I've been telling myself since I decided to take the job at the school that *this* isn't why I returned to Pike's End. That I didn't come back to feel Asa's mouth on mine again. To have him fuck it, conquer it, own it. To overwhelm me with his taste, his hunger... him.

That I didn't return to finish what we started on the floor of his home two long years ago.

But I can no longer lie to myself as his long fingers tangle in my hair and hold me a willing prisoner for the ransacking of my mouth with his tongue, lips, and teeth.

This isn't the sole reason. But it's part of it.

Asa is part of it.

With a groan, he presses stinging, hot kisses to my cheek, temple, jaw. Then, before I can chase those beautiful lips, he's on his feet again and he doesn't wait for my fumbling attempts this time. He attacks his own jeans, ripping the button up and jerking the zipper down. But as he thrusts his hand inside the opening, I jerk out of the erotic stupor he's thrown me in and bat his hands away. Or rather, he allows me to.

An urgency fueled by too many nights filled with sweaty, dark dreams drives me, and I pull the band of his black boxer briefs back with one hand and dip inside with the other. I don't hesitate. Hesitation is for those who don't have a ticking clock hanging over their heads. For those who have never known what it is to have their heart's desire snatched from them in a blink of an eye. So no, I close my fist around him as if this is my hundredth time touching him, squeezing him, stroking him, not my first.

And maybe it is. If I count my dreams.

My lids lower and I luxuriate in sensation. In the feeling of hot satin over hard steel. Of strength and vulnerability in my hand. At the musky, delicious sandalwood-and-earth scent that's more condensed, headier here. Unable to prevent myself—and because I can—I lean forward, pressing my nose to the black cotton of the boxer briefs, inhaling. But it's not enough. I tug the underwear down, and my pussy contracts at the sight of my smaller hand curled around his thick, long cock. The Batmobile with Gotham's favorite vigilante could come tearing right through my living room and the commotion couldn't drag my enthralled attention away from my fist sliding up, up, up his length, closing over the dark-red, plum-shaped head. Couldn't rival how bruised and angry that wide cap appears as a bead of pre-cum glistens at the slit, lubricating my palm for the glide back down.

Inhaling that alluring male fragrance isn't enough. Not with my tongue heavy in my mouth and my breath breaking on my parted lips like gasped prayers.

I need to taste him.

Angling him toward me, I sink my head over his cock, taking him into my mouth. Swallowing him as deep as I'm able.

"Fuck, India," he snaps, his hands gripping the sides of my head. His snarl vibrates in the air above me as his cock bumps the back of my throat. "Baby girl, hold the fuck up."

But I can't. It's almost as if I'm in a trance, drowning in lust, in him. I draw back, his girth sliding over my tongue. My lips close over the head and I give it a strong, healthy suck, laving the tip, teasing the slit. The salty musk has me humming and instantly addictive, and I return for more. Always more. That's what got me on my knees in the first place. The insatiable quest for more. Tilting my head forward, I tongue the underside of the flared cap, and his hold on my head tightens, sending prickles of almost pain scattering across my scalp.

"Goddammit, India." The warning is evident in his lust-thickened voice.

"Don't stop me," I murmur, vaguely surprised by the rasp in my own tone. I almost don't recognize it, having never heard it before. Drunk. I sound damn near drunk, and it's on need, on Asa. Brushing a kiss over his damp skin, I dip my head and drag my tongue up his length. "Let me have this. Have you."

"Then take it. Stop teasing and take it. Fuck this dick like you mean it." He sounds mean and something else. Almost... desperate. And I understand that. I *feel* that.

Once more, my lips part and I suck, lick, yes, fuck his cock. Like I mean it. It's messy. It's wild. I put all of me to work jacking him off. My head, mouth, tongue, hands. If I could wrap my whole damn body around his dick, I would. And his growls, moans, and filthy words of praise encourage me to take more, go farther. When the tip bumps the back of my throat again, I breathe deep through my nose, then exhale, allowing him to enter. And when his big body tenses, each furious curse is my reward.

So I do it again.

And again.

And again.

He cups my throat even as the other hand remains in my hair, steadying me, holding me in place as he takes over. I drop my hands and cradle his bare hips as they piston back and forth, his cock gliding over my tongue, hitting my throat and breaching it with every thrust.

"So good, baby girl," he grunts, his thumb stroking the front of my neck. "So fucking good." His nostrils flare and for a moment, his grip tautens on both my neck and hair. "I'm coming. Let me know if I need to pull back. Now. Otherwise, I'm filling you up."

I answer by shifting my hands to his ass and digging my fingernails into the dense muscle.

With a groan, he snaps his hips forward, burying his cock in my mouth. Again and again. And then, on a muted roar, he's pumping his cum into my mouth, down my throat. I swallow, greedily accepting all he's giving me. And when he shudders against me, I lick and suck his slightly softening cock, coaxing for a little more.

"Fuck," he rasps. "Fuck."

He cradles my face between his big palms, his breath harsh puffs that serrate the air. For long moments, his eyes close and only his chest rises and falls. When his lashes lift several seconds later, the need in them hasn't dimmed. If anything, it's intensified. And it leaves me lightheaded. Excitement and anxiety flutter beneath my navel.

"Where's your bedroom?" he whispers.

"Down the hall." I jerk my head in the direction of the shadowed corridor, my voice just as hushed.

He curves his hands beneath my arms, gently but firmly pulling me to my feet—then he sweeps me off my feet. Winding my arms around his neck, I brush my lips over the base of his neck, flicking his inked skin with my tongue, teasing his racing pulse. And taking more than a little pleasure than I'm the cause of that rapid pace.

He doesn't ask for any more help in seeking out my bedroom. With unerring accuracy, he locates the darkened room and enters, heading straight for the tidily made bed. Asa settles me on the mattress and rounds the side of it to switch on the lamp. His gaze surveys the large room with its cedar armoire, the small sitting area with the armchair, ottoman, the tall, thrift-store-find cheval mirror in the far corner, and finally the bedside tables, before returning to the huge, hand-carved sleigh bed. And me.

Wordlessly, he stalks the few steps back to me, reaching over his head and grabbing a fistful of his shirt and yanking it up and off in that way that's flagrantly masculine and so goddamn hot. My lungs constrict, cutting off all air as his wide, hard, tattooed chest comes into view. He's... beautiful. All that black, red, and dark-blue ink covering his chest, arms, and neck—he's wild, raw, and so gorgeous, I close my eyes for a moment. As if that will allow me to ground myself for a second. But no. It only magnifies the slight ache in my jaw, and the phantom possession of my mouth. Reminds me that he's had a part of me already, and my pussy throbs to be owned, too.

When he reaches me, he encircles my ankles, tugging me to very edge of the mattress. Silently, he quickly strips my jeans and panties from me, and only when I'm naked from the waist down does he lower his piercing gaze from mine to my wet, desperate sex. A sound that seems half growl, half moan rumbles out of him and falls to his knees, hiking my legs over his shoulders, spreading me wide.

Mortification. That's what should be swamping me right now. This man is face deep in my pussy and staring at my folds like I'm the Holy Grail and he's about to drink until he sees God. Modesty whispers in my ear that I should at least make an attempt at shielding myself, but that would be a lie. But I decided tonight there would be no lies, and that includes not deceiving myself either. I'm not embarrassed. I love the way he looks at me. Crave it.

He wants to feast on me, and *God*, I want to be devoured.

As if he discerns my thoughts, his gaze flickers up

to meet mine as those long, blunt-tipped fingers spread my swollen, feminine lips. A whimper escapes me, and even I can hear the hunger in it. I'm not embarrassed by that either.

His head lowers, and I can't look away as his mouth opens over me. And devastates me.

That wicked mouth licks and sucks at my pussy, leaving no part of me untouched, uncorrupted. He licks at my folds, sucking each one into his mouth, lapping at it, nibbling, leaving me shaking even before he travels up to my clit. By the time he circles the engorged bundle of nerves, *I'm* one exposed nerve. My fingers tangle in his hair, clutching him to me. Sweat pours off me, my body trembles. As his lips close over my clit, and he thrusts the side of his tongue against it, I cry out, pushed so far to the edge, insanity is a real possibility if he doesn't let me come.

"Don't you fucking come," he growls, and the vibration of it shivers through my sex. "Not yet. Not until I say."

Part of my mind says *fuck that*. But my body is under his thrall. Though the need to fall into the abyss, to let go, claws at me like a wild beast, I hold back, knowing the pleasure already careening through me like a runaway train with greased wheels will be nothing compared to what he can give me. What he will give me.

He slides two fingers through my soaked folds, the tips nudging my clit and I groan, flinching from the bite of pleasure that tips into pain. It's damn near too much. That groan melts into a whimper when he dips his hand to the grasping entrance of sex, and I pull my knees higher, pressing the soles of my feet onto his shoulders.

"Please," I beg, past caring. That's a lie. I never cared in the first place. "Asa, please, give it to me."

"You never have to beg me, baby girl."

He's a man of his word. With one thrust, his thick fingers fill me, stretch me, and my back arches off the bed. My hands fist the bedcovers beneath me. But my hips twist and buck, fucking those fingers. I'm on fire—it's in my blood, and I can't control it. I'm in danger of burning up and taking this man, this damn house with me.

"That's it." His dark chuckle brushes my damp inner thigh. "That's it. Show me how you get there."

Another low laugh, and then a heavy arm crosses my hips, and he holds me down, shoving his shoulders higher between my thighs, spreading me wider. He plunges his fingers inside me, shoving me toward release, and I can't do anything but lie there and take it. With each thrust, he crooks his fingers, rubbing a spot high inside me and I choke, squirming, trying to get closer or get away from the immense pleasure that's building with each rub.

"Where you going?" he teases with a dirty chuckle. "Where you going, baby girl?"

Another stroke, another rub, and I have my answer.

I'm flying. I'm shattering.

I'm not sure if I'll be whole again. And I don't care.

When I open my eyes moments—or maybe minutes, hours, eons—later, Asa crouches over me, completely naked. I discover it isn't just his chest, arms, and neck that are tattooed. His thighs and calves are inked as well. Half-naked, he was beautiful. Wild. Completely nude, he's almost overwhelming. And though I've just had the most cataclysmic orgasm of my life, already my senses are winking back online.

Lust reignites in my veins, and I stretch my arms toward him.

Asa straightens, catching my hands and helping me to sit. With swift movements, he removes my shirt and bra, rendering me as naked as him. Bowing his head, he kisses me, and though it's brief, it's still hot, carnal, and has me clutching his shoulders.

"You still with me?" he asks against my lips. "If this is where you want this to end, it can. But you need to speak up now."

"After you get me naked?" I twist my lips into a wry smile.

"I'm hedging my bets." There's humor in his voice, his eyes, but there's also strain around his mouth, and his fist drops to his cock, and I can't help but watch as he squeezes it, strokes it.

I slick my tongue over my lips. "No fair," I whisper.

"I never said I would play fair." He pinches my chin with the hand not busy jacking himself off. "India. I need an answer."

"I want you inside me. No." I shake my head, lifting my hands to his hair, running my fingers through the thick, silken strands. "I *need* you inside me."

Before I can draw in my next breath, my head is against my pillow and he's over me, opening a condom package then rolling the protection down his cock. I shiver, staring at it, a spasm quivering deep and high inside my pussy. Like in the hall, a flicker of feminine anxiety flutters in my belly. He's going to stretch the hell out of me, and since it's been a while between partners, this might be uncomfortable at first. But it's worth it. To have him finally buried inside me? It'll all be worth it.

"What're you thinking?"

I jerk my gaze from his cock up to his face and that dove-gray gaze.

"It's been a minute," I admit.

Something flashes in his eyes.

"Define 'a minute.'"

"A year."

He studies me, then shifts closer, cupping my cheek with one hand and lifting my leg over his hip with the other. His cockhead nudges my pussy, pressing against my entrance.

"Your pace, baby girl. Your say-so." He rubs his thumb over my lips then leans down and grazes his mouth over mine. "Tell me when."

"When." I wind my arms around his neck, burrowing my face in the crook between his shoulder and neck. "Please."

He doesn't make me wait.

Asa thrusts, and I stiffen. No, I hadn't been wrong. He's... huge. Almost too huge. Only the head and a couple of inches are inside me and I'm trembling. My pussy ripples around his cock, and he holds still above me, letting me become accustomed to him.

Yes, it's been a year, but this... this is different. I've never been this full. This stretched. This branded. And he's not finished. There's more of him. I nearly tell him *never mind*. Nearly. But I sink my teeth into my bottom lip. Because I want all of him. I want to be completely filled by him. I long to be conquered and to conquer.

"India?" he rasps into my ear.

I shake my head, not sure what he asking right now.

"Don't stop."

"Baby—"

"Don't. Stop."

Tunnelling his fingers through my curls, he yanks my head back out of his shoulder, peers down in my face as if he needs to ascertain the truth there for himself. Then, slamming his mouth down over mine, he thrusts his tongue between my lips just as he drags his hips back and slams them forward.

I scream into his mouth. He swallows it, not lifting his head, taking it, continuing to kiss me, fuck my mouth even as he sits fully seated inside me.

His dick throbs within me, and I'm caught on a tenuous hook of pleasure and pain. And pain has the edge. I can't relax, my breath a loud buzzsaw in the room.

"Shh."

He continually kisses me, soothing me. He cups my breasts, sweeping his thumbs over my nipples, circling them before dipping his head and sucking the tips into his mouth. Fierce pleasure arced from my breasts to my sex, tiny, electrified bolts attacking my pussy, and I cry out with it.

Soon, the pain ebbs and I'm writhing beneath him, legs cradling his hips, ankles riding the small of his back.

"Asa, please. Move."

Skimming a hand down my spine to cup my ass, he lifts me to him, and a hard smile curls a corner of his mouth.

"Whatever you say, baby girl."

And he *moves*.

He draws his hips back, his dick dragging over tiny feminine muscles, lighting me up, until only the tip remains inside me. Then he drives forward, propelling the breath out of me. I'm lit up like a torch. Pleasure blasts through me, and if I wasn't already on my back, I would've tumbled there, blinking, shocked, utterly derailed. What is he doing to me? What is he doing to my world?

I didn't sign up for this.

Part of me feels like he should apologize for completely wrecking me.

But there won't be any apologies coming.

At least not until he's finished this beautiful destruction he's started.

Rearing back, he slides his other hand under my ass, splays me out over his thighs and fucks me in earnest. I can do nothing but grasp the covers beneath me and hold on. Throw myself at his mercy and let myself be broken on the waves of ecstasy.

With a groan that originates from my soul, I allow myself to be broken, to be used, to be worshipped. Because that's what he's doing. Each time he buries himself inside me, reshaping my pussy so only his dick will fit, he's corrupting me and revering me. I'm his sinner and his goddess.

"Touch those gorgeous tits," he says, and not waiting for me to obey, he grasps my wrists and raises my hands to my breasts. "Let me watch you play with them."

I close my eyes, my fingers pinching and tweaking my nipples, plumping my breasts. My back arches, lust a living thing inhabiting me. Only he could get me to do this. To *be* this.

"That's it." His fingers slip over my stretched folds, wetting them, then he rubs my clit.

Oh fuck.

I can't. I *can't*.

"Yes, you can," he says in a firm tone that he me racing to an edge that there's no backing away from. I hadn't been aware I'd voiced the words aloud. "*Now*, India."

I detonate. Implode.

Above me, he continues to thrust, to stroke, to fuck me into oblivion, and I'm dimly aware of his roar as he throbs, filling the condom. But I'm too far flung, too far gone.

But before the darkness closes over me, a whisper of unease whispers across my soul.

There's no going back.

7

Asa

"Ms. Colleen, I haven't had food like that since..." Jessie leans back in his chair and shrugs, grinning. "Well, since the last time I was here and you cooked for me. Thank you. No one spoils me like you do."

"Go on, boy." Mom picks up his plate, lightly slapping him in the shoulder with her free hand. "I'm not believing that charm or that smile. I've seen both on TV. And besides, I bet you say pretty much the same to your own ma."

I snort. She might claim not to believe him, but her red-stained cheeks are declaring something else. As if she can read my thoughts, she glares at me, bumping my shoulder as she grabs my plate, too.

"Now, you know my mother doesn't cook, Ms. Colleen." Jessie laughs. He shakes his head. "She can organize the hell out of a garden party, though."

"Well, we all have our talents. Don't go getting on your ma like that. How is she, by the way?" my mom asks, pausing at the dining room door.

Jessie shrugs again, his grin dimming just a bit,

though his voice remains as upbeat as before. "She's fine. Staying busy with the beginning of the holiday season. It means more benefits, social events, and galas, and social events and galas to support the benefits. Anything as an excuse for her and Dad not to spend time in each other's company, but continue to stay married."

And that doesn't come across as bitter at all.

Mom tries to cover her wince, but doesn't quite achieve it. As long as Jessie and I have been friends, we've been aware of his less than... *ideal* home life. Yes, he grew up in a two-parent home where he wanted for nothing, every need met even before he asked for it. But there were certain things missing in his house that I had in spades, in spite of growing up with a single mom, where making ends meet was akin to an Olympic sport. I had love. Affection. Acceptance. When Jessie had loaned me the money to open up my shop, we'd argued about me paying back; he hadn't wanted my money. According to him, Mona and Mom and I opening our home to him had been a gift he would always be grateful for.

So many people looked at him, the great Jessie Reynolds, with his high-class, wealthy, educated background, his illustrious football career, his current great sportscaster job... they looked at him and only saw who and what they wanted to perceive. Surface. A handsome successful, golden boy, who couldn't seem to do any wrong. But they didn't see the lonely, emotionally and often physically abandoned boy and man, who replaced feelings with things, with accomplishments. The man who fucked up because *happy* scared the shit out of him. The man who sought to do better, to be better for those who loved him, more than for himself.

"I love you, you knucklehead," Mom says, then pushes through the swinging dining room door.

His smile, this time, warms and is more genuine.

"She likes me more than you." He waves a hand in the direction Mom just disappeared.

"Probably." I lift my coffee cup, sip. "Shit. Definitely."

He laughs and picks up his own mug and takes a sip. Rubbing a hand through his hair, he sighs and jerks his chin up. "Hey, I could've used a wingman last night. Where'd you disappear to?"

I freeze. Guilt and fear curdle in my gut like spoiled milk.

Guilt, because memories of exactly where I spent last night flash across my mind. With those images, lust licks at the underside of my skin, pumps through my veins. But I don't need those visions to still feel the vise grip of India's too tight, soaking wet, and goddamn perfect pussy on my cock. To inhale her jasmine, fresh rain, and hot sex scent off her skin. To hear those breathy moans and throaty whimpers that signal her pleasure and need. I don't require reminders of any of that, because they're all emblazoned on my mind. And that only deepens the guilt.

Fear, because I'm afraid my betrayal is stamped on my face in permanent ink, easy for him to read. I feel like it is. Hell, when he showed up on Mom's doorstep for the breakfast we prearranged, I longed to duck my head, terrified he'd take one look at me and know. Know that I'd crossed a line in our friendship.

"Nothing," I say, shocked the answer emerges steady, normal. "I just went home. It was a long day." *Fuck*. I'm just digging a fucking deeper hole by lying to my best friend. "Why? What did you need a wingman for?"

His mouth twists into a rueful smile. "To keep me from drinking just enough to do something incredibly stupid, like find out India's address and go over there and beg her to give me another chance."

The bottom of my stomach plummets into a free fall. Holy shit. If he'd done that...

"Looks like you didn't need my help after all," I manage, taking another sip of coffee to do something with my hands and wet my suddenly arid throat. "What'd you end up doing?"

That smile hardens into something harder, though the regret lingers. "Not what. Who."

I stare at him, blink. Blink again. Because surely... Slowly, I lower my cup to the table.

"Excuse me? You fucked someone last night?"

"Can you please—" He throws a look over his shoulder toward the dining room door. "—keep your voice down? And yeah. Tracy. From the bar." He scrubs his hand over his hair again and heaves a hard breath. "After you left, I stayed and had a few more drinks and we ended up talking. A lot. I hung around 'til closing and followed her home."

I can't stop staring at him. My thoughts tumble in my head like a big-ass jigsaw puzzle with missing pieces. Shock has me by the throat, threatening to choke me out.

But even at the frozen edges of it flickers the red flames of anger.

Is he fucking kidding me?

"Let me get this straight," I say, leaning back in my chair, crossing my arms. "Last night, you see India for the first time in two years. The first time after you fucked up by falling on your dick into another woman."

"Asa," he grumbles.

"No, let me finish." I hold up a hand, palm out before tucking it back under my arm. "You see her again, not only ask for her forgiveness, but you beg her for another chance to be together. You tell her you still love her. And then, not hours later, you're fucking another woman? What the fuck, Jessie?"

"Yeah, what the fuck?" he snaps, damn near slapping his coffee cup to the table. A little of the brew sloshes over, but he doesn't notice, all of his frustration and irritation are focused on me. "India's the one who said she doesn't want anything to do with us being together again. She doesn't even want a friendship, and she damn sure isn't in love with me. Do I still love her? Yes. But what do you want me to do? Spend two more years pining after a woman who can barely stand to be within three feet of me? She says she doesn't hate me, but she must, to not even send me a fucking text in two years letting me know she's alive." His nostrils flare and his harsh breaths punctuate the silence in the room. "So yeah, I went home with Tracy. I used her to forget that the woman I love could give a single solitary fuck about me. I'm not proud of it, but don't sit there and judge me either, Asa."

I struggle not to; I can see his side.

But then I put myself in his shoes.

If India had told me *no*, I wouldn't fold and go bury my dick in another female. I'd probably get blind fucking drunk, then figure out how to win her back. How to change my damn self so I'm worthy of a woman like her. To fucking *beg* her to not shut the door but to leave it cracked. Something other than what Jessie did... again.

"I wish you hadn't told me," I murmur. "India and I... we're..."

"India and you are what?" Jessie asks sharply, his eyes narrowing. "What the fuck are you, Asa?"

Wish the hell I knew. Fuck buddies. One-time lovers. More than friends.

She's the woman I've always longed for, but could never have because she belonged to you first. First and always.

"We're friends," I quietly say instead of all the replies rushing through my head. "Since she's become Rose's vice principal, we've grown to be friends." And this feels like a lie of omission. A-fucking-gain.

"With one big difference. We're not together. And according to her, she doesn't give a damn," he says, bitterness coating his tone. "So your conscience is clear."

My conscience clear? Yeah, not so much.

My sins went back two years and were as recent as last night. Absolution wasn't coming to me anytime soon.

Especially not from my best friend.

8

India

Lena leans around the doorframe of my office, her long dreads swinging over her shoulder.

"Hey, India, if you don't need anything else, I'm going to head out. There's a BOGO sale over at that new shoe store in the outlet mall with my name all over it."

Smiling, I wave a hand at the administrative assistant. "Of course, go. And thank you for coming in. I really appreciate you sacrificing a couple of hours on your Saturday for me."

I hadn't asked Lena to give me a hand in gathering the teachers' lessons plans and organizing them so I could review and make notes on them. But when she called and found out I would be over at the school, she volunteered to come on in. And I'm thankful. What's the saying? Two hands are better than one? And it's definitely less lonely and she makes the work easier. I have digital copies of the plans as well just in case—God forbid—the Department of Education request an audit but for bi-weekly purposes, I print the lesson plans out and critique them.

"Believe me, it's no problem at all." Giving me a wave, she disappears from the doorway and I hear her moving in the outer office. "See you Monday!"

"Bye! Have a good weekend!"

I bow my head over the lesson plan on my desk, making a note in the column about the comprehension section of Ms. Dillon's language arts class, when a soft noise from the Lena's office caught my attention.

Smiling, I call out to her. "What did you forget?"

"Apparently, my mind. Morals. Sense of self-preservation."

Shock reverberates through me, and I stiffen, my fingers clenching around my pen so tight, it's in danger of snapping.

That most definitely is not Lena.

Inhaling a deep, deliberate breath, I lift my head. And meet Asa's gaze.

Like a light switch, desire floods me at just the sight of him. At the memory of what he'd done to me, to my body the night before.

But an instant later, reality doused some of that electrified heat. Reality in the form of remembering waking up alone this morning. That happened when the person you've gone to sleep with snuck out at some point in the early hours like a thief.

Or a guilt-ridden cheat.

"What're you doing here?" I ask, and my calm tone belies the thud of my heart against my sternum.

"You." He moves into my office, hands stuffed in the front pockets of his jeans. "I went by your house, but when I didn't see your car there, I drove here on the off chance you'd be here. I called the office to reach you and spoke with the office assistant. The one with the glasses and shit-eating grin? She didn't say anything?"

Wait until I get my hands on Lena. I'm kicking her ass.

"No," I say through gritted teeth. "She must've forgot to mention it."

He shrugs a muscled shoulder. "She's the one who let me in on her way out."

Of course she did. I'm *so* kicking her ass.

"Okay, that explains the how, but not the why or what. Take your pick."

Yes, my voice holds all the warmth of the Arctic winds, and if there's any justice in this world, he's freezing his nuts off right now. I'd known going into last night that I would regret it. Not being with him—I could never harbor any remorse over touching him, kissing him, having him inside of me. Finally. No, I would regret that strained, uncertain aftermath, when we struggled to look each other in the eye. When he wallowed in his shame and saw me as a walking, breathing betrayal, instead of a woman he claimed to desire.

Little did I know he wouldn't even stick around for the walk of shame.

He leans his big frame against one of my bookshelves and studies me. It calls on every scrap of pride I can scrounge to hike my chin up and continue meeting his gaze. But I need him to say whatever it is he came here to say, and get out.

One lesson I've learned lately? When it comes to this man my pride is an endangered species.

But I've done this before. I've been here before.

And I'm not willing to revert to that version of myself. Not for Asa. Not for lo—

What the hell?

My heart pounds, and my temples drum with the incessant thundering beat.

I refuse to be one of those people who get some good dick, then suddenly believe there's something more to their feelings other than residual lust. Hearts in their eyes, hell. Not unless they're penis-shaped.

"What, Asa?" I press, pinching the bridge of my nose and tossing my pen to the desk. "I don't speak strong, silent type. Can you say whatever it is you stalked me to say, then go? I have work to do."

"Stalked you?" He snorts then gives his chin a short dip. "To be fair, this is Pike's End. You can't drive from one end of the town to the other without seeing everything and everyone, so I would've seen your car here eventually." He pauses. "I came here to apologize for leaving you alone this morning. I'd left Rose with Mom, and had arranged to have breakfast over there."

"I assume with Jessie," I add. "Speaking of, does he know you're here now?"

"Yes, with Jessie. And no, he's spending the day with his parents at some event." He cocks his head. "India. We agreed to meet up at Mom's before he even arrived in town. This morning had nothing to do with last night."

Like hell. "Okay."

"Okay." He stares at me, eyes narrowed. "Just like that." He shakes his head. "Why don't I believe that it's so easy?"

"What do you want me to do, Asa? Yell? Throw my stapler at you? Last night was last night. A one-time thing. I went in with my eyes wide open, knowing where I stand with you. Nothing changed from yesterday to today." I smile, and it feels grim on my lips. "Besides, I just received this stapler from the school. God knows the next time I'll receive one. I'm not wasting it by throwing it at you."

"You went into it knowing where you stand with

me," he slowly repeats. "Enlighten me, India." He pushes off the bookshelf. "Where exactly do you stand?"

I scoff, but inside... inside my lungs have decided now is as good a time as any to take a vacation. My pulse hurls itself against the base of my throat like a caged wild thing, determined to make a jail break.

"Are we really doing this?" I rise from my chair, flattening my palms on the desktop.

"Yeah, do it, baby girl," he rumbles, and dammit, heat explodes to life inside me, licking at my nipples, belly, my pussy. That issued challenge is gasoline on a fire that never truly banks.

"Fine." I straighten and meet those molten silver eyes, even though I yearn for nothing more than to glance away while ushering him out of my office so I can lose myself in work and forget him. Forget that even though I knew better, I let him... hurt me. "I had sex with you last night, aware that I would be your dirty little secret. And when you snuck out of my house, *my bed,* so Jessie wouldn't be suspicious that you spent the evening somewhere else—like with his ex—you confirmed that."

"You're right."

My lips snap shut, and I blink at him. He stalks closer until his thighs push against the edge of my desk and he leans forward into my space.

"You're right," he repeats, firmer, grimmer. "I left without waking you on purpose. Yeah, I did sneak out. Because I'm a fucking coward when it comes to you. You're—" he broke off as sharply as a twig being snapped by a vicious wind. His jaw works for a moment, a muscle ticking along the side of it. "You terrify me. Everything about you. I'm scared to look at you and reveal just what the fuck it is you do to me when I have no business feeling this for you." He pauses and his gaze sears past skin, bone, and tissue to the soul of me. "Had no business feeling when you belonged to a man I called friend."

Holy shit.

Ice crackles along my veins, transforming me into a block of ice. Yes, we kissed that night I discovered Jessie cheated on me, but that's not what Asa's statement implied. From what he said, he desired me *before* it all went to hell.

"Yeah." Asa nods, the corner of his mouth lifting in a smile that isn't one. "You heard right. The reason I could kiss you, touch you that night you came by my house is because I'd been fantasizing about doing just that for years."

"But you..." I shake my head, then clear my throat of the hoarseness. "You could barely stand to look at me. I thought you only tolerated me for Jessie's sake. And now you're saying..."

"That I'm a damn good actor." He snorts. "Yeah." He frowns, thrusting his fingers through his hair and dragging the chin-length strands out of his face. "Me leaving this morning without saying anything had nothing to do with you and everything to do with me afraid to wake you up and see the regret in your eyes. Or hear the 'that was a mistake' speech. Putting off both a little longer when I still had your scent on my skin became my short-term goal. So I got out of there like a little bitch. But India." He stretches an arm across the desk and pinches my chin. Sparks ignite and pop from the skin-to-skin point of contact. "There's one thing you're wrong about. You could never be my dirty secret. Ever. I'd leave you alone first before I demeaned you like that."

"Maybe not intentionally," I whisper, his hold on

me rendering my resistance to him the consistency of tissue paper. Any second now I'm going to tell him to remove his hand. To not touch me. Any second... "I don't believe for a moment that you'd ever purposefully do that, Asa. But in your blind devotion and loyalty to Jessie? In your guilt for wanting me?" I smile, and it's as humorless as his was. "Tell me the truth. At breakfast this morning, did you tell Jessie where you spent the night?" His full lips flatten and his grip on my chin tightens. It's all the answer I need. Circling his wrist, I tug on it and tilt my head back, freeing my head from his grasp. "Just because you don't volunteer the truth doesn't make it any less of a lie. Any less of a deliberate secret."

"What I'm trying to do is avoid hurting my friend. Shit," he growls. Pivoting on his heel, he strides across my office, scrubbing a hand over the nape of his neck. "I'm trying to avoid hurting everyone."

Including you?

The questions shimmers in my head, and I'm shaken by it. And in that instant, I'm caught between rounding the desk, charging over to him and wrapping my arms around him, and asking—no, demanding—he leave. For my sake. For my heart's sake. Because it's a foolish, stubborn, unreliable thing, and even now, it's trembling in a stupid bid to throw itself at the toes of his scarred boots.

If what he said about concealing his secret... *crush* is the wrong word. What happened last night with his face between my thighs didn't feel like a "crush." But if he's wanted me since Jessie and I were dating, then he's had a long time to perfect a wall, a façade of indifference. And a person only did that to protect themselves. I ache to hold him, tell him it's okay to let go.

That I won't use whatever he shows me, shares with me, against him.

One the other hand... On the other hand, my own sense of self-preservation urges me to run. Run as fast as I can and don't look back, because those eyes, that face of stark angles and harsh beauty will surely reel me back in.

And only one thing exists down that path. Losing myself in a man only to lose myself.

Again.

"Well, you can't," I murmur. "One of the first lessons you learn as a teacher is you can't save every student. And it's arrogance to believe you can."

He turns, studies me, expression inscrutable. "Doesn't mean you don't try."

I nod. "Just as long as you know when to step back and let go. If not, you both will go under."

We stare at one another for several long moments, then I drop my gaze to the desk and pick up my pen.

"I need to get back to work," I say, avoiding that scrutiny that's as heavy as a hand wrapped around my throat.

"India."

"No, Asa. I understand why you left—believe me, I do. I also get that you're trying to protect everyone in a difficult situation. But I can't be a casualty to your friendship anymore. Before, you didn't owe me anything. Now?" I curl my fingers around the pen, briefly closing my eyes, unable to voice the pain, the damage it would inflict to watch him relegate me to an afterthought. A problem to be handled. "I promised myself I wouldn't harm myself again. And I won't let you do it either."

His frown reappeared, fierce and furious. "I'd never hurt you. Do you really think so little of me—"

"You already did this morning," I whisper. And his head jerks back, his expression blanking. "You should go, Asa."

His big body quivers with tension, and for a moment, I think he's going to deny my request and storm around the desk. And if he did that... God help me, I don't know if I would be able to resist him.

But I won't have to find out.

He ends up giving me an abrupt nod and leaving. Taking the air in the room with him like a huge vacuum. With a shuddering sigh, I sink into the chair behind me, clutching the chair's arms. Revelations from our conversation whirl in my head.

Asa wants me—has for a long time—but he won't let himself have me. With his body, yes. But where it matters? I'll never be his.

And he'll never be mine.

Because both of us will always be Jessie's.

9

Asa

I crack open Rose's bedroom door and peek inside. Rose lies sprawled under her yellow and white bedcover, her leg and arm flung to one side, her red curls spread like fire across her pillow. A soft snore echoes in the room, and I smile in spite of the weight pressing down on my chest.

It's become a habit of mine, looking in on her about an hour or so after her bedtime. Hell, I think I've gotten better. Right after Mona died, I'd slip in here and sit beside Rose's bed for hours, making sure she still breathed. Yeah, I might've stuck a finger under her nose a time or two. Losing my sister did a number on my head. One I'm not over, if I'm honest with myself. I fear there will always be a hole in my heart for her. But having her daughter here helps. At first, being Rose's guardian might've scared the shit out of me. Still, there's a measure of peace, knowing I'm caring for and raising the person Mona loved most in this world. Even if gray hairs are imminent.

I gently close the door and head down the hall toward the stairs. My smile fades as I descend the steps and walk into the living room. Sighing, I sink onto the couch, and the weight that's been with me since this morning resettles on my shoulders.

I hurt India.

I fucking hurt India.

By trying to keep the peace, to protect Jessie and her, I brought pain right to her door. I did that shit. It's all on me. Closing my eyes, I fall against the back of the couch, rubbing the heels of my hands into my eyes.

Somehow I had to make this right—

A knock on the front door snatches me from my dark spiral of thoughts. Shoving to my feet, I walk toward the door, frowning. I'd told Jessie I wasn't up for company tonight. Far as I knew, he intended on spending another evening with Tracy. And Mom had a rousing night of bid whist planned with Aunt Billie and several of their friends. Unless something came up at the garage and it's Jake...

There's only one way to find out.

I twist the lock and, grasping the knob, pull the door open.

And stare.

"Asa," India quietly says. "I'm sorry for showing up without calling ahead. Is it okay to drop by?"

I understand what she's asking. Is the coast clear? Is Jessie here?

"Yeah." I step back, jerking my chin. "Come in."

How I managed to get those words past my constricted throat is a minor miracle. Shock has a vise grip on my throat, and I briefly close my eyes, inhaling her fresh, seductive scent as she passes by me. I lock down the groan that scrambles up my chest as my body switches online, requiring only her presence to power on like a switch. Fisting one hand at my side, I close and lock the door with the other.

India turns, glances towards the staircase.

"Rose?"

"Asleep. Come into the living room." I walk past her, careful not to intrude on her personal space, even though she showed up here at ten o'clock. "Once she's knocked out, it would take a natural disaster to wake her, but I don't want to try it."

I don't look over my shoulder, but it's not necessary. I can *feel* her.

"Make me understand."

Now I look at her. I need to. Turning around, I study her, take in what had escaped me when she first walked through my door. The shadows in her brown eyes, the tipped down corners of her bare, lush mouth, the stiff gait that replaced her usually fluid, graceful stride.

"What's wrong?" I demand, tamping down the instinctive, roaring need to go to her and pull her close. "What's happened?"

She shakes her head, holding up a hand even though he didn't move toward her. At least he didn't think he did.

"Nothing. Everything." She huffed out a soft, dry laugh. "I've spent all day trying to forget what you said today. Trying to forget... you." She shrugs and looses another of those bone-dry, humorless chuckles. "But I can't. I can't get you out of my head. You'd think after two damn years, I'd realize what a pointless endeavor that it is, but I guess hope springs eternal, right?"

You'd think after two damn years, I'd realize what a pointless endeavor that it is...

"Two years," I rasp. "You've thought about me for *two years*?"

Her lashes lower, and she bites her lower lip. My heartbeat is a cannon in my ears because it doesn't seem as if she's going to give me the answer I need more than my next breath.

I'm ready to drop to my knees and beg for that answer when she murmurs, "Yes."

"Why did you run?" I demand.

"You know why."

Impatience crawls through me and I slash a hand through the air. "Why did you stay away? For *two fucking years*."

But she shakes her head, her dark curls grazing her shoulders. "No, your turn, Asa. Make me understand." She repeats the request she initially made when arrived.

An emotion spasms across her face, but it's there and gone so quickly, it's impossible to decipher. Doesn't stop me from deliberately locking my muscles to prevent me from crossing the distance separating us and hauling her against me. And holding her to make sure that emotion doesn't appear again.

"My father skipped out before I was old enough to remember what a piece of deadbeat shit he was. My mother died—and yes, logically I know she didn't want to leave me, but death is still a form of abandonment. And sixteen-year-olds don't really understand why they shouldn't be angry with the dead. Hell, there are some days the twenty-six-year-old doesn't either."

"India," I breathe, my palms itching to stroke her hair, her back, soothe and comfort her in any way I can. That she'll allow.

"Jessie might as well as have abandoned me," she

continues. "His actions killed our relationship, leaving me adrift, confused and so alone. And now there's you, Asa. As much as I want to believe differently, I know there will come a day when you'll walk away, too. It'll be the day when you're forced to choose between me and a friendship with Jessie." She pauses, and *Christ*—she's killing me. Not just that accusation that strikes too close to home. Those penny-brown eyes so full of shadows, full of hurt, are shredding me. "So make me understand the bond that demands such loyalty and devotion, so at least when I'm staring at your back after this," she waves a hand between us, "implodes, I get why."

It's on the tip of my tongue to deny her claim, to refute that I'll walk away from her. Be another person to abandon her. But she won't believe me. I can see it in her eyes. So all I can give her is another truth she will accept—the one she came to my house to hear.

"Jessie and I have been friends for years. We met through being on the football team together in school, but our friendship surpassed that. You know about his home life. You may not know that he often escaped to my house for peace, to just be accepted for himself. I've seen the perfect, can't-do-no-wrong, golden Jessie that he shows the world. But I've also been privy to the imperfect, insecure, vulnerable Jessie that he hides from most people. I've been there for him—my family's been there for him—and he's done the same for me. I wouldn't have graduated if it hadn't been for him. Sports have always come easy for me, but the books? No. And he understood that if I were to get into college, it wasn't going to be by my grades. It was going to be how outstanding I was on that field. And I *had* to get into college because it was my only way into the

NFL. Jessie dragged my ass across that graduation stage by the skin of my teeth. I couldn't have done it without him. As a matter of fact, I've never asked, but I'm not completely convinced, he didn't have his father pull some strings and make it happen."

She jerks and surprise flares in her eyes. Yeah, I've never admitted that to anyone. Not even to Jessie. We've never talked about it. Maybe I didn't bring it up with him because I don't want to confirm that it's true. Maybe I need to hold onto that sliver of doubt that it's not. Still, I promised myself I would be honest. Even if it didn't show me in the most flattering light.

"We went to college together, planned to enter the draft together. And when my football career ended during my second year in college, he was right there beside me. He didn't give up on me even when I gave up on myself. When I had to rediscover who I was without football. And he gave me the loan to start up my business. I wouldn't be where I am today without him. No bank worth a damn would've given me a loan —my credit was fucked, and I had the business experience but not the college degree. I owe Jessie. Not just for being my best friend. But for being my lifeline."

"Who can compare with that?" she whispers.

I huff out a short, serrated laugh that scratches my throat. "You don't get it, do you?" There's no fucking way I can't *not* touch her any longer. Striding forward, I'm pulling her into my arms, and thank fuck she doesn't resist my embrace. My hands stroke up her back, and I curl one over her shoulder and the other around the nape of her neck. "That's why I've fought so hard to keep my hands off you."

I press my mouth to her ear and absorb the shiver that ripples through her body. Her hands lift between us and press at my chest. To push me away? To just touch me? I don't know, but this grinding need within me decides which team it's on, and I lean into her palms, her long, slim fingers. A groan rumbles out of me, and that shiver runs through her again. She's killing me.

I tighten my hold on the back of her neck.

"You are the only woman who could make me risk that friendship, that loyalty. But that didn't just start since you returned here to Pike's End. I've known since we first met. Since you became my best friend's woman. I've stood by, the worst kind of man, watching you two fall in love, knowing you were giving him this perfect little body, and I hated myself. Because I already betrayed my friend by wanting his girl. And I knew if you'd look at me once with those beautiful brown eyes the way you did at him..." I trail off, graze my teeth over the rim of her ear and follow the outer shell with my tongue. Her whimper squeezes my cock like the sweetest, dirtiest caress. "This has been my existence for years. You. I have been, and continue to be, wrapped up in you. For two years, I lived half a life because you were missing. Even when you were with my best friend, at least I was able to just *be* in your orbit. Get my fix, even as it tormented me. Even knowing I'd come crawling back for another one."

I lean back, cradling her face between my palms and tilting it back. Fuck, she's gorgeous.

"India, Jessie might've been my lifeline, but you could so easily be my life."

She closes her eyes, and her hands shift from my chest to my wrists, encircling them and holding on.

"Asa," she breathes.

"Look at me."

I wait, outwardly patient, but inside... Shit, inside, my heart attempts to kick a hole through my rib cage. I've just admitted to her my years-long obsession, and she hasn't run away screaming in disgust. Yet. I brace myself for what I'll glimpse in her eyes. Shock? Horror? Wariness? Pity? God! I'd rather see the disgust in her gaze than pity. I can deal with her not returning even an iota of the same feelings for me, but not that.

Her lashes lift, and... relief and unfiltered joy pours through me, and my hold on her face tightens, but I can't loosen it. I can't let go.

There's lust there, yeah. But there's... more. I'm afraid to identify the more. Because if I'm wrong...

I bend my head and take her mouth in a raw, wild, probably bruising kiss.

Slow down. Easy, a voice whispers in my head. But I stifle that voice because I can't afford slow or easy. Not when there's a chance that *something* I spied in her eyes might disappear in the next instant.

Or when there's a chance that my fevered, desperate mind might have imagined it.

Thrusting my tongue between her parted lips, I moan, both in relief and ravenous hunger, when she opens wider for me, surrendering to me. She gives me another of those little, hot sounds of need, and I lap it up, swallow it down in greedy bites. And go back for more. Always more with her, because I'm never satisfied.

I'm beginning to fear I'll never be satisfied.

Releasing her face, I shove her jacket off her shoulders, then strip her sweater over her head, throwing it to the floor. Her bra joins the clothing seconds later. On a growl that tears out of me, I cup her breasts, squeezing them, shaping them. Fuck, she feels good. Like a goddamn miracle.

Her fingers tighten on my wrists like cuffs, and her head tips back on her shoulders. Her teeth sink into her bottom lip, and her body shifts in this restless movement akin to a dance. This is India adrift in passion, letting it consume her. And it's humbling that she has never held back her pleasure from me. Has been uninhibited with me. She's trusted me with her body.

Now I want more.

I want her heart.

I press my forehead to her chest, right over said organ.

My stomach knots, recognizing and understanding the consequences the pursuit of her will bring. The bomb it will detonate in the relationships in my life—well, just one in particular. And that scares me.

But not having this—not being able to touch her, inhale her jasmine-infused skin, kiss her smooth, brown skin—scares me even more.

That desperation claws at me again, harder now, leaving deep furrows, drawing emotional blood. The urge to mark her, to claim her, wells within me, and I draw her nipple into my mouth, sucking hard, flicking the beaded tip with my tongue. Her hands tunnel through my hair, nails scratching my scalp, scattering pricks of pleasure/pain in their wake. With a moan, I curl my tongue around her, pull harder, and twist and roll the other tip between my fingers.

Fire blazes through my body, lust a relentless task master, a demanding boss. And I obey. Willingly. Switching breasts, I treat the neglected flesh to my mouth, tongue, and teeth, eliciting shudder after shudder from her. My cock aches, pounds, and I grind it against the soft give of her belly, seeking some kind of ease. But it's fruitless. The kind of alleviation I need can only be found in that sweet, hot, tight pussy.

And I have to get in there.

With a hunger that borders on obsession, I have to get deep inside her.

Once more, I claim her mouth while my hands drop to her joggers. In moments, I've pushed them and her panties down her legs, removing the clothing and her sneakers out of the way. My breath saws out of my chest as I stand before this goddess in all her glory.

Belatedly—shit, what does that say about me as an uncle—I remember my niece sleeping upstairs—I cup her hips and move her farther into the living room.

As if she recalls Rose, too, she shakes her head, her hands going to my chest. "Rose?" she whispers.

"Asleep," I say. "And nothing short of an atomic bomb is waking her up. But come here." I maneuver her around the end of the couch, away from the room's entrance. Turning her so she's facing the sofa's arm, I curve an arm around her waist and slide the other up her torso, between her breasts, my fingers splayed across her collar bone. "Kiss me."

She turns her head, resting it on my shoulder, and giving me her mouth. I slip my hand over her hip and between her thighs, finding her soaking wet.

"Goddamn, baby girl," I growl against her lips, nipping the full bottom curve. "All of this is for me?" Palming her pussy, I thrust two fingers inside her, and those slick, firm walls quiver around me. My cock throbs in complaint. "Tell me, India. This is mine?"

I'm wading into dangerous territory, skimming a crumbling, creaky ledge that, if I were smart, I'd back away from before I tumbled over it.

But I don't heed that warning. Instead, I thrust harder, press the heel of my palm against her clit and circle it. She pants into my mouth, and I circle harder, press harder, thrust harder.

"Is this mine?" I ask her again.

"Yes," she whines, gasping when I slam my fingers back into her. "Take it, Asa. Take me. Please."

How is it possible to get greedier for her, more ravenous? It's an ache in my gut, and only she can satisfy it. I capture her mouth, fucking it, and slide my hands free of her. She's all over me, and I lift my head, slipping my fingers between my lips and licking her off my skin. Her taste hits me like a runaway train, and I close my eyes, savoring her musky, delicious flavor. And as seems to be my theme with her, it's not enough.

I grope at the front of my jeans, jerking the button open and the zipper down.

"Shit," I mutter, pressing my forehead to her shoulder. "Wait here. Don't move."

I shift away from her. My condoms are up in my bedroom since I didn't expect company tonight. I'm going to break the sound barrier running up those stairs and to my room—

"Hold on." Her smaller hand clasps mine, stopping me. She stares at me, her lashes momentarily lowering before lifting and her eyes meet mine again. "I've never been with anyone without a condom. Never. I've never trusted anyone that much. I want to have this first with you."

I go still. But the lust inside me rages like a rabid beast, hammering and beating against its cage, which happens to be my bones and skin. She wants *me* inside her. *Bare*. Nothing between us.

Oh fuck.

"Yes," I ground out, and *yes*, it emerges as if my voice had been chewed up in a woodchipper and spit out, but I don't care. "I'm clean, baby girl. And the thought of sinking in you, feeling nothing but you..." I loose a groan, and cross the very short distance back to her, covering her mouth with mine. In seconds, I have my fist wrapped around my cock, just shoving my jeans down and out of my way. "Take me in, India," I say.

Plead.

She reaches back and between us and guides me to her... into her.

I hiss as I sink inside her pussy. It was just last night since we were together, and I've missed this. Missed that initial resistance then surrender. The wet heat. The vise-like grip. The firm suction. It's the closest I've come to heaven. And if it's hell, I don't want my soul to be redeemed.

Curving a hand around the nape of her neck, I press her forward and stroke my palm down her spine, cradling her hip. Staring down at the place where I'm lost, where I'm home, I draw back, watching how my cock glistens with her wet, feeling and hearing how her pussy reluctantly frees me. With a moan, I plunge forward, branding on my brain the sight of her taking me, swallowing me whole, just in case something happens and I can't have this anymore.

Over and over, I pull back only to drive forward, riding her, attempting to brand myself on her sex, her body, and her heart. With every thrust, every one of her muted cries, the lust whipping and tearing at me screams louder, threatening to rip me apart. I need to come, to let go. But not without her.

Slipping a hand over her hip and between her hips and the arm of the couch, I rub a fingertip over her clit. She writhes against me, and I don't let up, following her, circling, caressing... pinching.

She goes off, exploding, her pussy clamping down on my cock, milking me, dragging my release from me. For several more strokes, I hold on, ensuring she receives all that she needs. Deserves. Then, on that last piston into her tight-as-fuck sex, I free fall after her.

Knowing at the bottom, we'll catch each other.

10

India

"I wish you could stay." Asa's low, rough murmur brushes my ear. "I want you to stay."

I glance over my shoulder, and though I left his bed not ten minutes ago, just meeting those dove grey eyes sets off sparks on kindling that's always ready to be set aflame when I'm in this man's presence.

I want you to stay.

For someone who's been abandoned, denied, and betrayed, those words are pure temptation. My heart yearns to reach out for it, to trust it. But my head... my head that remembers every single time I've been left behind, that I've been devastated, warns me to be cautious.

The simple truth is I'm afraid to trust Asa.

With my body, my pleasure? To not physically hurt me or violate the boundaries I set? Yes. All day I trust him with those. But with my heart? The hope that keeps trying to climb in my chest and take root? No? For him, there isn't a world where he can have both me and his friendship with Jessie. I don't know if it's possible either, but there's a part of me that's willing to find out. But Asa? Regardless of what he said last night —regardless of how he broke my chest open with hope—I still have zero doubts who will always be his first priority.

Jessie. Not me.

And I promised myself that I would never settle again. Never reduce myself so someone else could feel comfortable, important, or worthy, rendering me none of them.

Yet...

Yet, I want to stay.

I want to believe.

I want to be his.

"Considering I'm Rose's vice principal, and if she wakes up and sees me here, it'll be all over the school on Monday, I think it's best I leave now," I drawl, shrugging into my jacket.

"Yeah, she has no filter." He huffs out a short chuckle. "She won't do it on purpose, but she will spread our business faster than an STD in a frat house."

I scrunch up my nose. "Nice."

"India." He shifts to my side, cups my face. "It doesn't stop me from wanting it. Tomorrow, okay? Tomorrow, we need to talk. Really talk."

"Tomorrow is today," I whisper.

"Yes." A smile ghosts across his lips. "Today then. We'll talk today."

I nod, though my pulse crashes in my veins, under my skin.

"Today."

He pinches my chin, tilting my head back. When his mouth claims mine, I close my eyes, luxuriating in his taste, in the texture of his sensual, firm lips, in the erotic play of his tongue. It would be a very tragic thing if he ever suspected how much he owned me.

Releasing me, he reaches behind me, twisting the lock and grabbing the knob. A hard pebble of dread takes up residence between my ribs, and part of me almost turns around and marches back up those stairs to the sex-scented sanctuary of Asa's bedroom. But I step back, and as he pulls the door open, I dismiss that kernel of unease. It's ridiculous—

"Oh shit, you scared me." Jessie laughed, a key dangling from his fingers. "I was coming by to crash on... your..."

Ice slithers through me, coating my veins, my organs, my very blood. And as Jessie's stunned gaze collides with mine then jerks to Asa, I'm left frozen, unable to move, unable to escape this horrible scene that has been set on a collision course from the moment we kissed two years ago.

"What the fuck is this?" he demands, his voice growing louder with each word until he's nearly shouting.

"Keep your voice down," Asa growls, the gentle touch on the small of my back belying the fierce frown darkening his face. He ushers me out of the house, forcing Jessie back off the front stoop and down the stairs. Once we're at the end of the walk, he stops. "I get we're going to have this out, but my niece is in that house." He jerks a thumb over his shoulder. "So keep your damn voice down so you don't upset her."

Jessie glances at the house, and though the fury doesn't abandon his expression, when he speaks, his tone is lower. The anger, though. The anger saturates every syllable.

"You're so concerned about Rose, but unless I'm reading this shit wrong," he rotates a finger back and forth between me and Asa, "you were in there fucking where she's sleeping. So make that shit make sense."

"Don't do that, Jessie," Asa says, and the quiet warning in those words, coupled with the stillness of his large frame, send a shiver coursing through me. "Don't go so far you can't walk it back. Now, if you want to address what's in front of you, we can do that. But leave Rose out of it."

Jessie's lips flatten, and he glances away, a muscle jumping along his clenched jaw. After a moment, he turns back, and his gaze jumps from Asa to me, then returns to Asa.

"How long has this been going on? Or do I want to know?" he asks, the corner of his lip curling in a sneer. "Have I been apologizing for a mistake I made two years ago, when all along you two were fucking around behind my back?"

"No." And standing so close to him, the slight flinch that jerks his body reverberates through me. "I would never betray you like that."

"You'd never betray me?" Jessie's sharp crack of laughter echoes in the early morning air. "What do you call this?" He waves a hand toward me.

"This?" I speak up for the first time since Asa opened his front door, a spark of anger melting the numbness that had encased me. "I'm not a *this* or a *situation*, Jessie. And whatever is between me and Asa doesn't have anything to do with you."

"You don't think so?" His sneer turned uglier. "I don't know if this is some revenge fantasy of yours, India, but you're not naïve and I'm not stupid. So please don't pull that 'believe me, not your lying eyes' bullshit. Is this your way of getting back at me? Getting with my best friend? Trying to come between us? Well played, sweetheart."

This *asshole*. Shock punches me in the chest, momentarily robbing me of breath and speech. Is that really what he thinks of me? Believes I'm capable of? Hurt swirls with fury, merging into a murky, whirling mass.

"You have your fucking nerve," I whisper. "*You* broke us. You did that all on your own. I was a good partner, a faithful partner. So whoever I move on to or with is my choice and my business—and sorry to break this to you, Jessie, but you don't have a say in it. More importantly, there isn't a stamp anywhere on my body that says, 'Property of Jessie Reynolds.' You don't have a claim or a right to me. Only I have that." I drag in a shaky deep breath, and his lips part as if to reply, but I'm not finished. I slap up a hand, palm out. "Now, maybe it's in your character to do something as underhanded, as spiteful to use another person in some petty plot that's two years in the making, but let me disabuse you of that notion—that's not me. Mainly because you ceased being that important to my life two years ago. You don't add to it, you don't take away from it."

His eyes narrow even more, and his nostrils flare. With jerky movements, he turns his body away from me and faces Asa.

"You crossed a line—you know you did. It's why you didn't say anything to me before now. You have a choice to make. Her or me." Jessie throws down the ultimatum, and under the hard, crystallized fury, I catch the confidence. As if he's already certain of Asa's decision.

And the kernel of dread that took root in my chest just before we left his house, sprouts roots, curling in and out of my rib cage.

Because I'm sure of his decision, too. I always have

been. Shame on me for letting myself believe for a second that the outcome could be different.

Even before Asa looks at me, I brace myself for what's coming. But I'm kidding myself. It would be like Noah's neighbors preparing themselves for a flood. My world is about to be rocked, and all I can do is stand here, climb to higher ground, and try to survive as long as possible.

"India, we'll talk later today," he says, that low, silk-over-gravel voice firm. No, not firm. Final.

I shake my head, a fissure zigzagging through me, leaving cracks and crevices in its wake. But damn if I'll break in front of these two men. I've given both of them pieces of me—Jessie, in the past, and Asa as recently as minutes ago. And both of them tossed me away as if I were disposable, expendable. And I guess I am to them. Bros before hoes, and all that.

I huff out a serrated laugh that abrades my throat, and Asa's gaze narrows on me.

"India," he says.

"No." I shuffle back a step, away from him. From Jessie. From this dynamic that I became tangled up in like a sticky spider's web. And I have no one to blame but myself. I entered it with my eyes wide open, foolishly believing I could control the traitorous organ pumping away in my chest. One day I would learn. Maybe the pain racing through me like wildfire would be enough to brand this lesson into my soul and head once and for all. "Don't worry, Asa. I got it. We won't need to have that talk. I understand perfectly, and further conversation isn't needed or wanted. I don't want... any of it."

He claims one of the steps I surrendered, his grey eyes nearly black in the early morning darkness. If possible, his frown is fiercer, and the bold lines of his face stand out under his skin in stark relief.

"What the hell are you talking about? I'm telling you, I'll see you later today."

"And I'm telling you don't bother." I hike my chin up, going for strong, trying to gather the last scraps of my pride around me, but they're so tattered, it's a damn near futile effort. "I'm out," I say, slapping my hands together and holding the palms out. "I vowed to never again let anyone make me question my worth. As much as I—" the *love you* lodges in my throat, and I refuse to free it, "—care for you, I owe myself more than that. I deserve more than that. And if you can't see it, than you don't deserve me."

I don't spare Jessie a glance or any more words because, like I told him, this isn't about him. He isn't the one causing my heart to squeeze so tight, I fear my knees hitting the pavement before I can make it to my car.

No, that honor belongs to his best friend.

The man who offered me false hope that maybe, just maybe, there could be an *us*.

That I could be Asa's girl.

11

Asa

I stare after India's retreating figure, and though I'm physically here, still solid, my bones feel brittle. As if one careless touch will send me crumbling to the ground.

She's gone.

Doesn't matter that I can still see her, and within seconds I could catch up with her before she reached her car—she's gone. She might as well be across the fucking country. Or vanished again. Lost to me.

Everything in me roars in protest, demands that I follow her *now*, not tomorrow. Not another goddamn minute. But I can't. Even though I damn near tremble with the effort of not going after her, and my fucking bones ache with the need to do just that, I turn back to my best friend.

Because he's owed an explanation. After years of loyalty, of unconditional love and acceptance, the very least I can give him is that—I *owe* him that. And if we are to walk away from each other with any semblance of a friendship, I need to try.

"Are you serious, Asa? Of all the women you could've fucked, why her? Why India?" Jessie rasps. "I know it's a ridiculous question, but while you were getting your dick wet, did you think of me at all? Of our friendship and how you were blowing it up over a quick fu—?"

"Watch your mouth," I snap. "You're angry, and you're justified. With me. Not her. But don't expect me to stand here and let you disrespect her."

"Oh, so you're her knight in shining armor now?" he laughs, and it's ugly, but there's hurt, there's confusion swirling beneath. "While you've cast yourself in the role of the great protector, did it occur to you to protect our friendship? I thought of you like a brother..."

He shakes his head, letting the rest of the sentence trail off, and my sternum constricts. *I thought...* Past tense. Pain bursts in my gut as if a phantom fist plowed into it. I'd expected Jessie to consider our friendship over. How couldn't I? Still, hearing it... I drag in a low, deliberate breath, but each inhale is like swallowing glass.

"I'm still your brother, regardless of how you think of me," I say, not shocked that my voice sounds like churned up gravel. "And to answer your question, yes. I always thought of you. Always. Which is why I kept my silence and my distance from India for years—including while you were with her. My love for you would never allow me to go there."

He stares at me, eyes widening. For a moment, his lips work but no words emerge. Then he swallows, his Adam's apple bobbing in his throat. "You wanted India when she and I..." When I give him an abrupt nod, he tunnels his fingers through his hair, fisting the strands.

"You're either a fucking fantastic actor or got a great poker face, because I never guessed." His face hardens an instant later. "So what'd you do, wait until I fucked up to shoot your shot? Was it you who told her about that groupie?"

My chin jerks towards my neck, anger, and yeah, guilt swarming inside me like a drone of angry bees.

"You would say that to me?" Could he really think that of me? "Fuck no, I didn't do that. Time for you to be honest, Jessie. That woman wasn't the first one, and she for damn sure wouldn't have been the last. Don't play the injured party when you were screwing around on India for the last year of your relationship. You want to know why I started getting too busy to come to your games? Not because being there was too painful of a reminder of what could've been. No, it's because witnessing you fucking up the best thing that ever happened to you by falling into random pussy like it was a goddamn BOGO sale made me sick. And there I stood, willing to give my left nut for what you had. Not your career. Not your money. Not your health. Your woman." I shake my head, loosing a harsh bark of laughter. "You were a fool. A fucking fool. But no, I didn't tell her. One of your side chicks with ambitions of being the main one or hopes of being Instagram famous did that."

A heavy silence falls between us because we've never discussed this. Never touched the topic of his infidelity, instead treating the incident that destroyed his relationship with India like a one-off, when we both knew it wasn't. It was the visible tip of a large, hidden iceberg.

"But here's the whole truth, Jessie. The night India found out you cheated on her, she came to me to see if it was true or not. She read it on my face and cried in my arms. We ended up kissing. But that's as far as it went. Then I didn't hear from her for two years, same as you. We didn't become lovers until last night. And that was because of you. I rejected her two years ago, and I repeatedly pushed her away these last few weeks because of you. *You*, Jessie. My friend, my brother. Even though you treated your relationship like gum on the bottom of your shoe. But I'm through with that. I'm done."

"What do you mean, you're done?" He steps toward me, his hands curled into tight fists at his side.

His blue eyes flare with hot fury, and it should ignite fear inside me. Fear at losing him, our relationship. But there's just sadness. And relief. Not relief over the fractures that have sprung between us that may never heal. God, never that. But relief, that I no longer have to live a lie. My feelings for India are a storm in my soul—one without an outlet. And they're bruising me from the inside out. I want to... Why can't I...

God, I just want to live out loud.

For me. Just once.

All my life, I've worked and lived for my mother, my family, for Jessie, and now for Rose. And not once have I regretted my choices. Not fucking once. I'd do it again.

But even when India wasn't mine, in my heart, she was. And now, if she'll have me, I want to be hers. No more wasting time. No more putting my life on hold for others. No more existing in fear.

"I mean," I say, moving forward and clapping a hand on his shoulder. He flinches, jerking out from under my palm, and yeah, that hurts like hell, but I absorb it. "I mean, that I love you, Jessie, and I will always be your friend, whether you want to continue being mine or not. Everything you've meant to me, been to me, done for me... I'll never stop being there for you. But I won't deny how I feel about India any longer. It's more than fucking or wanting. I need her. Rose does, too. And I'm not walking away from her. I refuse to end up another name on that list. Not when—"

"You love her."

"Yeah," I whisper. "Yeah, I love her."

We stare at one another And I wish I saw acceptance or forgiveness in his eyes, his face. But I don't. There's pain, anger, even grief. But no, not forgiveness. I don't know if I'll ever have that from him. Or if we'll ever be who we once were.

And I'll have to find some way to be okay with that.

"I'll guess I'll head back to Connecticut," he murmurs.

Pain slashes across my chest in deep red grooves. "Jessie." I stretch out an arm. "Please, let's go—"

"Not now, Asa." He shuffles backward, hands up. His gaze shifts away from me as if he can't stand to look at me any longer, and fuck if that doesn't make me bleed harder. "I don't know... when. But definitely not now. Tell Rose I said hi. If it's cool with you, I'd still like to call her, check in on her. And your mom."

"Of course, man. You know that. I'd never—"

"Yeah, I have to go."

With that, he turned on his heel and strode away, leaving me alone in the steadily brightening morning. I wait until he climbs into his car and pulls away before pivoting and returning to my house where my niece sleeps. To my bedroom where my sheets still contain the scent of India and sex.

Sleep is a joke, and I cross to the window, watching the indigo slowly lighten to lilac and soft grey. It's not lost on me that as day dawns, promising fresh beginnings, my oldest friendship ends.

But maybe, just maybe, it means the start of a new one.

12

India

"India! India!"

I halt midstride toward my car in the teacher parking lot, and my eyes close. Pain streaks across my heart, a hot, bright-red ball of fire. But an instant later, I lift my lashes, paste a smile on my face, and turn around to face Rose.

After all, it's not her fault her uncle left me an emotional wasteland.

It's not her fault I did something as eternally dumb as fall in love with her uncle.

God, I'm such a cliché. Apparently, good dick did make me an idiot.

You know it's so much more than that.

Yes, I do, for once agreeing with the know-it-all voice in my head. That's the thing—it's never just been all about the sex with me and Asa. From the beginning, I ran to him because he'd always represented a solid, safe port with his quiet, stalwart strength. In a life where uncertainty and unreliability had been my "normal," his dedication to family, to the career he'd built out of the ashes of his dreams, even to Jessie, fed a greedy heart that had been deprived for so long. He's a protector of those he cares about.

But he just doesn't care enough. At least, not for me.

And that's okay. *I'll* be okay.

And eventually, if I keep telling myself that, I'll start to believe it.

"Hey, Rose," I greet the little girl. Arching an eyebrow, I take in her slightly lopsided braid, and suppress my reluctant smile. The braid actually looks better than Asa's earlier efforts. He must be watching those YouTube videos I sent him. "What're you doing here? Is everything okay?"

"Yes." The little girl launches herself at me, wrapping her arms around my waist. "I missed you. Where were you yesterday? I asked Ms. Hesche where you were but she said you didn't come to school. Uncle Asa was looking for you, too."

My heart seizes at the mention of Asa's name, and I try to keep the panic out of my voice as I pat her back. But there's nothing I can do about the barb-tipped knot lodged in my gut.

"Rose, you aren't over here by yourself, right? It's not safe to walk around unattended without an adult."

Please say your grandmother is with you. Please say your grandmother...

"No, Uncle Asa is here. There he is!" She twists her torso and points behind her.

Damn.

I can't *not* look up and in the direction she indicates. And my breath catches in my throat.

Asa stands several feet away, his hands jammed in the pockets of his jacket, his warm gaze settled on me, and it chases away the coolness of the October afternoon. I'm tempted to cross the parking lot, cuddle close to that wide chest and bask in that warmth. Let it burn away the sting of rejection, of hurt and insecurity.

But it's because I want him to take the pain away that I stay exactly where I am.

I may be a fool, but so far it's a closely kept secret. Letting him in on it doesn't appeal to me.

"Are you coming over to our house again, India?" Rose tugs on my waist, and I jerk my attention away from her uncle and refocus on her. "It's not movie night, but you can eat dinner with us and force Uncle Asa to watch a movie. He'll do it if you're there."

Lord, this girl. Asa had better be careful or she would run him ragged.

"I'm standing right here, and I heard that." That familiar deep voice rumbles through me, and I fight the urge to close my eyes again. To bask again. But I manage. "Now hurry up. Kayla's mom is waiting to take you over her house for a playdate. I'll pick you up about six."

"Fine," Rose mutters, loosening her arms from around my waist. She gives me a wave, a "Bye, India! See you at dinner!" even though I promised no such thing and rushes the few feet across the parking lot to jump into the backseat of an SUV.

Leaving me alone with Asa.

Not for long though.

I spin on my heel and head for my car.

"India." I don't stop. I *can't* stop. "India, please."

It's the "please" that ricochets through me and causes me to jerk to a halt. It's so rare to hear *that* word in *that* tone—that desperate tone—from this big, dominant, proud man, I immediately still. But my heart, that reckless, silly organ, pounds away, destroying any semblance of calm.

Asa appears in front of me, his grey eyes soft but shadowed.

Dammit, it's not fair.

The moment he sent me away Saturday night, every need, every craving, every... heartbeat for this man should've ceased. I shouldn't be standing here in this parking lot visually caressing the sharp angle of his cheekbones or the carnal curve of his wide, full mouth. I shouldn't want to stroke my palms over his broad shoulders and wide chest, shift between those powerful, thick thighs.

I inhale a deep breath and glance away from the impact of him.

"Will you look at me?" he murmurs.

I force myself to meet his grey eyes.

"This isn't really the appropriate place for this, Asa," I say. "We should probably do this later."

"I tried calling but you won't answer my phone calls. And you haven't been home since Sunday. I don't have any pride left to mind admitting that I'm desperate enough to wait after school and use my niece to ambush you into talking to me." He holds up an arm, then drops it, his fingers curling into a loose fist. "I'm not above it, and I have no shame in admitting it."

Okay.

I blink.

"I needed a break after..." My throat tightens around the words that would describe Saturday night so I twirl a hand, letting that suffice. "Lena let me stay with her for a couple of days."

I don't know why I'm telling him this—yes, I do. So he isn't left worried about my whereabouts. And as his big shoulders ease down just a fraction, I'm okay with making that call. But that's the only allowance I'm willing to give. Because the longer I'm in his presence, the weaker my resolve becomes. Like ice cream left out in the summer sun, it's softening.

And I can't be that weak. Not again.

"I won't hold you up long, India," he says, his gaze roaming over my face as if he's trying to imprint my image on his mind. "I just have two things to say to you. First, I apologize for asking you to leave the way I did Saturday night—Sunday morning. In hindsight, I could've walked you to your car or taken you to the side and explained why I wanted you away from there. But now I get how you would've only heard 'leave.'"

He lifts an arm again, and once more I think he's going to reach for me, touch me. And I brace for it. Wondering if I will lean into his hand or step back to avoid it. But in the end, he thrusts his fingers through his hair, fisting the dark auburn strands.

"What you took as me abandoning you and choosing my relationship with Jessie over you was actually me trying to salvage whatever I could of that friendship. Because after I told him that I refused to give you up, I knew chances were we wouldn't have much of one left. But I needed to protect you from his temper and his mouth."

Wait, wait. He refused to give me up?

"I could defend myself, Asa." Although... damn. Because he refused to give me up. I can't let that go.

"You think I don't know that? You're one of the strongest women I know. But if he made one more ugly comment to you, we wouldn't have had a friendship to save. I hate to say it like this, but you were a distraction. As long as he could focus on you, he didn't have to confront the fact that he fucked up and had ownership in what was unfolding in front of him. That's the only reason I asked you to leave. I meant it when I said I'd call you later. I tried. I tried to find you, India. To explain. But I couldn't find you."

No, because I'd been in hiding, licking my wounds, shoring up my armor.

"You said two things," I whisper.

"Right." He nods. "I love you."

I blink. Stare at him. Blink again.

"What?" I rasp.

"I love you." Only when he says, "Yes, India, I do," do I realize that I'm shaking my head.

This time when he lifts his arms and reaches for me, there's no equivocation about what to do. I can't move. I can barely think. His large palms cradle my face, tipping my head back, and the armor I'd reinforced takes several hits, leaving it dented. But instead of pockmarked and scratched from rejection and pain, it's from hope and faith and love.

And they're more dangerous than any of the others.

"Asa," I cuff his wrists, not sure if I'm hanging on or about to tug him away. "I can't..."

"Yes, you can," he insists, and there's a vein of steel running through his words that brooks no argument. "You can trust me not to abandon you. You can believe in my word that I will always have your back and make you and Rose my priorities. You can rely on my love being a firm foundation for you to stand on or a springboard for you to fly from. I want to be whoever, whatever you need. Just as long as I get to love you, India."

I drop my armor. I don't need it. Not with this man. I ran to him two years ago, and now, I'm through running. For the first time since returning to Pike's End, I'm truly... home.

Turning my face into his palm, I press my lips to his skin.

"I love you, Asa," I murmur against his hand. "Say it again."

"I love you, baby girl." He tilts my head back so I'm looking into his pretty gray eyes, and if I harbored any doubts, one glance there melts any lingering uncertainties. This beautiful male loves me. Chooses me. "Your turn." He presses his lips to mine. "Say it again."

"I love you." I smile. "Now, I believe there was mention of dinner and a movie night."

He snorts. "She better be glad I would do anything to get you home with me. Including being played."

I laugh, and bending his head, he claims both my kiss and my laughter.

Home. I'm going home with him and Rose. Right where I belong. I might have started this journey two years ago as Jessie's girl, but now I'm all his.

All Asa's.

And he's mine.